AIRSHIP CITY

Stephen West

For my children

ONE

"Come on, Joey. Hand it over."

Joseph stared steadily at the speaker. *Don't be afraid of him,* he told himself. *He's just a kid like you. Even if he does dress like an organ grinder's monkey.* "I told you before, I don't have it. And it's Joseph, not Joey."

Mickey Cooper cracked a feral grin. "What do you think, lads? Does he look like a Joseph to you?" He stuck his thumbs in the pockets of his worn gold brocade waistcoat. His two companions regarded Joseph with open hostility.

"Nah, he looks like a Joey to me," said the one on his left, a weasel-faced boy with wisps of fuzz on his upper lip. The corner of his mouth lifted as he spoke. "A little runt."

Joseph snorted. "I'm a lot taller than you, Ned."

Ned flushed, his eyes narrowing in anger. "Oh yeah? Well maybe you are. But you ain't taller than our Tom, now are you?"

Joseph glanced at the hulking presence to Mickey's right. If Tom was taller, it was only by an inch or so. But he was massive, with a barrel chest and bull neck, whereas Joseph was beanpole-slim. Tom's dull eyes betrayed little emotion.

"All right, stop rabbiting on, you two! I don't want to hear

1

no more of your pony." Mickey's grin had disappeared, and he stared at Joseph with hard eyes. "I want that guinea, Samson, and I want it now!"

Joseph grinned derisively. "There haven't been guineas since before the Great War, Mickey. It's 1948. You should try to stay up to date."

"Oh I'm up to date all right, mate. But I thought I'd better ask you for something you could understand, what with you being a toff and all."

"I think I would understand you if you asked me for twenty shillings."

"It's twenty-one bob to the guinea. I want twenty-one, you hear?"

"I don't care if you say it's twenty-one or a hundred and twenty-one. You're not getting a penny out of me."

Mickey gave another of his mocking smiles, holding out his hands. "Look, Samson, I don't make the rules. Since before my time, the new recruits have been givin' a little something to the head clerk. Now it's your turn."

"Who made you the head clerk then? And since when has a little something been twenty shillings?"

Mickey's face turned murderous. "You don't know who you're messing with, Samson!"

"Actually I do," said Joseph with a sigh. "You want everyone to think you're some kind of gangster. But you're not hard. You're just a kid like the rest of us."

As suddenly as it had come, the hard look disappeared, and Mickey was grinning again. "Am I really? I don't think I'm the same as you. I didn't go to no Harrow School, f'rinstance." Ned laughed at this, a jeering laugh, and even Tom cracked a slight smile. Seemingly encouraged by this, Mickey turned to look at the rest of the office boys who were crowded in the post room of the bank. A ripple of nervous laughter started to work its way around the observing circle.

Joseph felt his cheeks starting to burn. "Well, I'm not there now, am I?" He hated the defensive tone in his voice. "Had to leave, when my dad died." He knew, as the words left his mouth, that he had made a mistake. There had been a slight quaver in his voice as he mentioned his father, and he steeled himself for the response.

It wasn't long in coming. "Oh dear," said Mickey, an awful parody of a concerned look on his spotty face. "I think we've upset young Joey here, lads." He looked at his companions. "Really, I'm ashamed of you two. Making fun of a boy who's lost his father." He turned his gaze back towards Joseph. "Go on then, Joey. Have a little cry."

The anger that always seemed to be just below the surface suddenly flared white-hot in Joseph, and he lashed out at Mickey. It wasn't a well-planned strike. Part of him seemed to watch his fist fly out in horror, afraid of the consequences. But another part, the part that had suddenly taken control, let out a roar of pure hatred, and drove his fist out blindly.

Mickey dodged it easily, though his eyes grew wide as his head bobbed back. Joseph's hand fastened itself to Mickey's neck, seemingly of its own volition. Mickey struck out with his fists, aiming to connect with Joseph's ribs, but his arms were too short to reach. Joseph stood there, holding the smaller boy off at arm's length as he flailed away.

This only served to make him more angry. Rage twisted his features as he roared dire threats at Joseph. But he was powerless to carry any of them out. Joseph felt his own anger subsiding, leaving him feeling scared and wondering what to do to get himself out of the situation.

But he was saved from having to decide when something hit him hard on the side of his head. He turned to see Tom's meaty fist withdrawing as the mailroom spun crazily, and its wooden floor suddenly rose up and hit him in the face.

Joseph was thinking how unfair it was for the floor to do that, as the jeers echoed dimly around him like the caws of crows, when all went suddenly silent. He twisted around to see what was going on, and looked up into the narrow face of Janice Honeywell, the office supervisor. She was regarding him with some concern in her eyes, which peered at him through enormous black spectacles.

"Are you all right, Samson?"

He managed to pull himself into a sitting position. His

head hurt badly, and he felt dizzy. "I think so, Miss Honeywell."

She frowned at him. "You don't look all right." He avoided her gaze, looking around the room. Everyone else seemed to have left. Almost everyone, that is. Ned was lurking behind the pigeon holes, weasel face scowling at him.

"What happened, Samson?" Miss Honeywell was insistent.

Joseph gave himself time to think of an answer by hauling himself laboriously to his feet. He steadied himself with a hand on a shelf. "I tripped, ma'am. Hit my head on the corner of the desk."

Miss Honeywell regarded him skeptically. She lowered her voice slightly. "If there's a problem— if you're being bullied — I can help you, you know. You can tell me the truth."

Joseph looked down at her earnest face. Prim and proper, buttoned up, secure in her authority here in the bank. What did that count for, out on the streets of the City or the East End? Would she follow him home tonight? Stop Mickey and his gang from beating him senseless? He looked away.

"I have told the truth, ma'am." He felt less dizzy. He stood up straighter, releasing his grip on the shelf.

Miss Honeywell stared at Joseph a moment or two longer, frown deepening. Then she sighed.

"Look, Joseph, I know it's not been easy for you. Things are not turning out the way you expected. But you mustn't give up hope. The world is changing, and there are new opportunities for young men, even if they haven't gone to university. You could still make something of your life."

Joseph nodded. "Yes, ma'am. Can I go now?"

Miss Honeywell rolled her eyes slightly. "Very well." But she was still watching him as he turned to go, and called out after him. "You'd better clean up that graze."

Joseph made his way unsteadily to the nearest toilet and washed his face in the basin, then examined his forehead in the mirror, brushing his thick black hair away to do so. The impact with Tom's huge fist had left an ugly red mark on his left temple, but above his right eyebrow the graze wept droplets of blood. He must have scraped it against a rough floorboard when he fell. Wincing as he dabbed at it with a piece of toilet paper, he stared at himself in the mirror, asking himself the question he had asked a thousand times in the past few months. *What am I doing here?* He still had no answer. He didn't belong in this place. The anger and frustration welled up inside him, so that he felt he might explode, or scream, or smash the mirror in front of him. He closed his eyes, taking a deep breath, and the moment passed. Sighing, he threw the toilet paper into the bin, and opened the door. He felt a bit steadier on his feet as he trudged back to the post room.

The rest of the day passed without incident, and when it was time to leave Joseph hurried out of the building and down the street, looking anxiously over his shoulder. But there was no sign of Mickey or his thugs, and he walked on with a growing sense of relief, which lasted almost all the way home. As he turned into the street where he lived, however, the familiar sinking feeling came over him. The sight of the dingy terraced house that was now his home was an unwelcome reminder of how much his life had changed after his father's death. He still hadn't gotten used to living here. In his mind, home was the pleasant red-brick house in Hampstead, with its green lawns and shady oaks.

He sighed, and walked up the narrow steps from the pavement, letting himself in with his key. To his surprise he heard voices from the parlour. Visitors were a rare thing in this new house. He stuck his head around the door and saw his mother sitting and talking with a strange man.

"Ah, here he is now," she said, rising and beckoning him into the room. "Joseph, I'd like you to meet Mr Monmouth."

The stranger stood and held out his hand. "Hello, Joseph," he said warmly. His grip was firm. "Get into a scrape at work?"

"Oh, you mean the graze? No sir," said Joseph quickly. He didn't want to alarm his mother. "Just tripped and fell."

"Of course you did," replied Monmouth, but there was a twinkle in his eye. He nodded knowingly as Joseph's mother fussed over him, peering up at his face.

"You must be more careful, Joseph." She turned to Monmouth. "I think he's grown too quickly, he's not used to his height. It makes him clumsy!"

"How tall are you, Joseph, six foot or so?"

"Yes sir." Joseph had learned that people automatically assumed that he would want to talk about his remarkable height. None of them ever seemed to realise that he might be tired of having the same conversation over and over again.

"And you're only sixteen! Still, I expect you hear the same thing from everyone. Must get boring, I suppose."

"Oh no, sir," said Joseph, so as not to appear rude, but he had to work hard to suppress a grin. Especially when Monmouth gave another knowing nod.

"Mr Monmouth knew your father," said his mother brightly, as she resumed her seat on the sofa. Joseph waited for Monmouth to sit down in the shabby armchair before sitting next to his mother.

"Yes, we worked together at the Zeppelin company. We were all very saddened by his death." Monmouth frowned deeply. "A terrible loss. He was an outstandingly gifted pilot. And a dear friend."

The silence lengthened uncomfortably, and when his mother sighed deeply, Monmouth seemed to rouse himself from his reverie. "I must apologise, Miriam, I did not mean to upset you."

His mother forced a smile. "No, Robert, it's quite all right. Would you like some more tea?"

"No thank you, and indeed I must be on my way." He stood briskly, picking up a black fedora from the side table. Joseph and his mother followed him to the door, where he paused on the threshold. "Thank you for the tea, Miriam." He turned to go, placing the fedora on his head, then turned back. "Joseph, would you like to meet me for lunch tomorrow, in the City? I've something to discuss with you that you might find very interesting."

TWO

"Well, what was all that about?" said his mother, as she closed the door behind Monmouth.

Joseph was just as puzzled. "I haven't a clue, Mum."

"Maybe he's going to offer you a job. Oh Joseph, promise me you'll never work for that awful Zeppelin company! I couldn't bear the worry if you started flying as well. You wouldn't do that to me, would you?"

Joseph stared at his mother's worry-drawn face. He understood her concerns, but her near-constant fear that he would suddenly decide to become a pilot could be tiresome. He forced a smile. "Of course not, Mum. Don't you worry, I've got a good job at the bank. Anyway, whatever Mr Monmouth wants to talk to me about, I'm sure it's nothing like that."

"So you work at the City and Empire Merchant Bank, do you?"

Monmouth sat back in his chair and puffed on his cigar, regarding Joseph through the clouds of smoke. They were in the dining room of his club. Their conversation had been limited to the weather (good) and the food (bad), but now it seemed that Monmouth would finally come to the point of their meeting.

"Yes sir, I work in the post room." He briefly wondered how Monmouth had known the name of his employer. *My mother must have mentioned it.*

"Ah." Monmouth had that slightly annoying half-smile on his face again. "Do you ever see Winston Churchill, I wonder?"

"I do sometimes, when I deliver his post." Joseph began to feel a bit uncomfortable about the questions, as if Monmouth were prying into something that didn't strictly speaking concern him. "Do you know Mr Churchill?"

Monmouth nodded. "Yes, I have met him. So you haven't sat in on any client meetings or anything like that?"

"No." Joseph now felt defensive, and then annoyed with himself for feeling that way. He was only sixteen, why would he be sitting in on client meetings? "I told you, I'm just a clerk."

"It's all right." Monmouth smiled encouragingly. "You can still help me."

"Help you with what?"

"Before we get into that, I'd like to talk about your father."

"My father? What does he have to do with it?"

Monmouth looked pained. He leaned forward, stubbing out his cigar, and glanced around before answering. When he did, he kept his voice low. "Joseph, there's no easy way to say this, but I believe that your father was murdered, and I need your help to bring his murderer to justice."

Joseph stared at him, shocked and stunned. "That's impossible," he said eventually. "My father was killed when his airship exploded. It was an accident, pure and simple."

"It was made to *seem* an accident." Monmouth shook his head. "But it wasn't. Ever since the *Hindenburg* nearly caught fire at Lakehurst, we have been absolutely dedicated to safety at the Zeppelin company. The moment I heard about the explosion, I *knew* it could not be a fault with the airship."

"So how was it done? Who do you think did it?"

Monmouth sat back in his chair. "I don't yet know exactly

how it was done. I've been following up clues and leads ever since the explosion. It's taken months and months of very hard work." He sighed, and rubbed his forehead. "Lots of dead ends, unfortunately. But just recently, I've had a bit of a breakthrough. I'm certain that Howard Hughes is involved in some way."

"You mean *the* Howard Hughes, the one who built Aeropolis? He's a client of the bank."

"Yes, I mean him. Hughes has been an enemy of the Zeppelin company for years, but I didn't think even he would go as far as murder. But now some new evidence has come to light. I need more information to confirm it, and I need you to get it for me."

Joseph was taken aback. "You need *me*? Why? What can I do?"

"You can tell me what Hughes gets up to when he comes to the bank tomorrow."

"How would that help you? Are you with the police?"

Monmouth shook his head. "No, I'm still helping the Zeppelin company. But now I'm with a special department, known as the ZA. We work to keep Zeppelin employees safe, and if needs be, we undertake investigations. I'm the head of investigations at the ZA."

Joseph grimaced at that. "Investigations, or spying? I'm not prepared to be a spy!"

Monmouth looked at him steadily. "It's not really spying. You're just going to tell me who Hughes meets, and so on. Just the sort of thing you might say to your mother, when you tell her about your day at work. Trust me, it will be a big help to me."

"I don't know. It still feels wrong, somehow. Like I'm betraying Mr Churchill."

"So Hughes is meeting with Churchill, is he?" Monmouth grinned. "You're helping me already!"

"I didn't say that!" Joseph felt a rush of panic. He hadn't known about the meeting, but Hughes had met with Churchill on previous visits. Now he had inadvertently given something away.

"It's all right, Joseph. No-one will ever know. Besides, you know what they say about ends and means, don't you?"

Joseph frowned. "I do, but I don't know that I agree with it."

"Well, agree with it or not, if you don't help me, you're effectively helping the man who killed your father to escape justice."

The words struck Joseph like a knife, cutting him to the quick. He felt a painful lump forming in his throat, and he wanted to cry out that he would never do that, never do such an awful, horrible thing. He felt tears starting in the corners of his eyes and he looked down quickly, swallowing hard, trying to control himself. He took a sip of water, noticing how his hand trembled slightly.

"Are you all right?"

He nodded back at Monmouth, not quite ready to speak again. Monmouth in response gave a concerned smile. "Why don't you think about it? We'll meet again in a few days, and if you want to tell me anything then, you'll do so. If not...." He shrugged.

Joseph had regained his composure, feeling grateful that Monmouth had not put further pressure on him. *I'll just bide my time, and tell him nothing when we meet again.* "All right. In a few days then." But there was a twinge of guilt there, when he thought about his father. Was he betraying him in some way, by not helping Monmouth? It was an awful dilemma, and it stayed with him through the rest of the meal, and on the walk back to the bank.

THREE

The familiar dread seemed to settle on his shoulders as he walked through the doors of the bank, and he looked anxiously around him for Mickey. He hurried through the wood-panelled corridors, the sound of his footsteps absorbed by the thick carpet. As he turned a corner he nearly ran into a portly gentleman who was smoking a large cigar.

"Mr Churchill! I'm so sorry!"

"Quite all right, dear boy," said Churchill, recovering his balance, and peering up at him. "My word, but you are a very tall young man! It's Joseph, isn't it? Joseph Samson?"

Joseph nodded. "Yes, sir."

"I knew your father, you know. Very sad to hear about what happened to him. He was a good man."

"Thank you, sir." Joseph stood awkwardly. He really ought to be getting back to the post room, as the meeting with Monmouth had taken him well over the allotted lunch hour. But the Chairman seemed to want to say more.

"Seeing you made me think of something, but now I've forgotten what it was." He frowned, pinching his lower lip. Then he suddenly snapped his fingers. "I've just remembered! Come with me to my office, I've something you might enjoy reading."

Joseph opened his mouth to demur, but Churchill had already turned to go back up the corridor. He followed the Chairman's surprisingly rapid progress, trying to avoid the cigar smoke wafting back. Presently they reached a pair of oak doors. Churchill flung them open and strode into his office, as his secretary jumped up from behind his desk in surprise and agitation.

"Mr Churchill, sir—"

"Not now, Pertwee," said Churchill, as he proceeded across the Persian carpet to his own enormous oak desk. He rifled through the papers and envelopes strewn across the green leather blotter. "Ah, here we are!" He picked something up and turned to Joseph with a flourish.

It was a copy of *Life* magazine. On the cover was a photograph of the city of New York, showing the Hudson River and lower Manhattan. Floating above the Statue of Liberty was an enormous airship, shaped like a silver doughnut. A forest of steel and glass towers rose up from the centre of a wide deck which covered the top of the doughnut.

"Is that… Aeropolis?" said Joseph.

"It most certainly is," said Churchill, smiling indulgently. "Would you like to borrow that, Joseph? I shan't have time to read it just yet. If you could let me have it back in a few days."

Joseph stared at the photograph, a mixture of emotions running through him. Airships and flying machines were anathema to his mother, being held responsible for his father's death, and he felt that he ought to hate them as well. But the shining aerial city in the image was so beautiful, it touched something deep inside him.

Churchill continued. "Well, I just thought… what with your father being a pilot and everything… that you would find it interesting."

"Thank you sir," said Joseph, shaking off his reverie, and stepping forward to accept the magazine. "It's very kind of you. I shall read it avidly." He nodded. "Please excuse me, sir,

I must get back to work."

As he headed down the corridor towards the post room, his eyes were drawn to the cover again. The image of Aeropolis was hypnotic, calling up a nameless longing, a promise of escape into a wide blue world of adventure.

He shook his head. *No, it's not for me. My mother wouldn't hear of it.* In any event, if what Monmouth had told him was true, then Howard Hughes, the creator of Aeropolis, was responsible for his father's death. He grimaced, rolling the magazine up in his hands. He certainly wouldn't be able to take it home with him, in any event. As he entered the post room, he tossed it into his pigeon hole, and turned to the pile of post from the afternoon delivery. He sorted through it quickly, and had just placed the last letter on its pile when he heard a familiar voice. His heart sank, but he forced himself to carry on and not respond as Mickey and his two sidekicks swaggered into the post room.

As Joseph picked up his sorted pile and turned to begin his rounds, he found his way blocked by the bulk of Tom, who stood staring at him impassively, arms folded across his barrel chest.

Joseph moved to walk around him, but the other boy sidestepped smoothly to prevent this. Joseph sighed.

"Mickey, could you get this great lump out of my way, please? I need to get these letters delivered."

"Oh, I don't think ole Tom's going to let you go anywhere until we sort out that guinea." Mickey's ridiculous waistcoat was today set off by a crimson silk cravat, and his face had a gloating expression on it. It made Joseph furious. He flung the pile of post back onto the table and rounded on his tormentor.

"When are you going to get it through your thick skull that I am NOT going to give you any MONEY!" he yelled. But Mickey just laughed.

"Temper temper, Samson." He stepped forward, lip curling in a sneer. "You want to keep on my good side, you do. I'm quite an important bloke around here. I could make things very uncomfortable for you." He leaned in until his face was inches from Joseph's. "I could even get you fired." His voice was virtually a whisper.

Joseph's stomach lurched. As much as he disliked his job, the thought of losing his meagre wage didn't bear thinking about. "You couldn't." He tried to say it with conviction, but his voice betrayed him. Mickey smiled thinly.

"Oh, I could. Suppose I told that stupid cow Honeywell to 'ave a butcher's at your pigeon hole, and she found a stolen banker's draft in there? She wouldn't take too kindly to that sort of behaviour, now would she?"

Joseph couldn't imagine that she would. Banker's drafts were similar to cheques, except that they were drawn on the bank itself. You could take a banker's draft into any other bank and it would be honoured, no questions asked. Stealing a banker's draft was essentially the same as stealing a large amount of money from the bank. Losing his job would be the least of his worries. He would in all likelihood go to prison if he were found in possession of a stolen draft.

Fear made a sick hollow feeling in his belly. He thought desperately, trying to find holes in Mickey's plan. "How would you get your hands on a draft? They're all locked away in Mr Pinborough's desk drawer." Joseph tried to speak with more confidence than he felt.

But Mickey just laughed. "Mostly they are. But ole Pinborough ain't the most careful geezer, in my experience. Might be he's careless with the key, one day." The evil grin returned. "Might be he has been already."

Mickey straightened up, pulling on his jacket lapels to straighten them. "So you'd best think about whether you want to show your respect for me, Samson. Best think really hard."

He jerked his head at Tom and Ned, and then strode out of the mailroom. They followed, leaving Joseph shaken and worried.

FOUR

Joseph was standing on a rooftop landing pad, somewhere in London. It was night, and a cold wind was blowing. An airship's dark bulk loomed above him. Gusts of wind struck its silver flank, making the fabric ripple slightly in the gleam of the moonlight.

Then from out of the shadows on the other side of the pad, a tall figure emerged. He was wearing a long leather flying coat, and he strode purposefully towards the entrance hatch of the gondola that was suspended beneath the airship's great envelope.

"Dad!" shouted Joseph. He started to run across the landing pad towards his father. "Dad! Wait for me!"

Morgan Samson stopped, and turned to look back at his son. He smiled, a soft, sad smile, and shook his head slowly.

"Wait for me, Dad! Please! Please wait!" Joseph was running as fast as he could, running with all of his might. But something was wrong. He wasn't getting any closer. He watched helplessly as his father turned and entered the gondola's hatch.

"Dad! Don't go! Wait for me!" Hot tears were rolling down Joseph's face now, as the airship dwindled in his vision, falling away from him, becoming smaller, until he couldn't make it out anymore.

He became conscious that he was lying in his bed, his pillow soaked with his tears, and knew the nightmare had returned. He lay there, the silence of the night all around him, and a familiar despair washed over him.

The unwelcome dream had been his nightly companion since the morning his mother, haggard and tear-stained, had awakened him with the news that his father had been killed in an airship explosion. For months it had tormented him, robbing him of sleep. The past few weeks had seen a slight respite, often with two or three peaceful nights in a row before the nightmare returned. But every time it did, he became afraid that it would get worse again.

Joseph rubbed his eyes and sat up, turning on his bedside light. He stared bleakly at the framed photograph on his nightstand. It showed a tall man in a leather flying coat, smiling at the camera. *Why did you leave us? I wasn't ready to say goodbye. I needed you. I still do.* Tears filled his eyes again as he felt the familiar, awful hollow pain in his chest.

He rolled away to face the wall, resigned to waiting until it was time to get up. He closed his eyes, even though he knew it would do no good, he wouldn't sleep again. He didn't want to anyway. The nightmare never returned a second time in the same night, but he was still afraid that it could…

"Joseph! It's eight o'clock! You'd better get up!"

His mother's voice awoke Joseph with a start. He sat up, confused, his heart pounding.

"Joseph! Get up now! You'll be late for work again!"

"All right, Mum!" Joseph yelled irritably. He felt tired. The memory of the nightmare came to him in a rush, followed by the recollection of Mickey's blackmail threat. And then he remembered the meeting with Monmouth, and the possibility that his father had in fact been murdered. He shook his head wearily. *I wake up from a nightmare into more nightmares.*

He hauled himself out of bed with a sigh, washed and

dressed, and plodded listlessly down the stairs and into the kitchen.

His mother turned to him as he entered. "Joseph Samson, you are sixteen years old! Your school days are behind you. Why do you make me run after you as if you were a baby? When are you going to take some responsibility?"

The unfairness of the accusation took Joseph's breath away. He had so much on his shoulders that he didn't know what to do about it. A quiet voice in his mind urged him to share his problems with his mother. But he knew he couldn't, he didn't want to worry her about his work, and as for Monmouth's accusations against Hughes, well, what was his mother supposed to make of that? He shook his head. He would have to deal with it all himself.

His mother was still looking at him expectantly. "Am I going to get an answer then?"

"Sorry, Mum. I didn't sleep very well."

Her expression softened. "The nightmare again? Poor Joseph." She reached up and ruffled his hair. "Well, sit down. I'll get your breakfast."

He sat down at the table. His mother scraped bacon and eggs out of the big cast iron frying pan and deposited them onto a plate. Glancing at the morning's copy of the *Times*, he took a sip of tea. The front page story was about Aeropolis. There was a large picture of the flying city, its elegant silver curves floating high above Big Ben, and the headline excitedly informed the world that "AEROPOLIS HAS ARRIVED IN LONDON".

He frowned, picking up the newspaper, and held it so that his mother couldn't see the front page. First the magazine that Churchill had given him, and now this. It was almost as if someone was deliberately trying to make his life more difficult. He read on, stealthily, about how Aeropolis had arrived in London only that morning, after a long transatlantic transition, and speculation as to the reasons for this were running high. Some senior City figures were quoted as saying...

The newspaper was snatched from his hands, and he

looked up into the worried face of his mother.

"Oh, Joseph, you're not reading about that horrible Aeropolis, are you? I just can't bear the thought of it, I'm so afraid you'll turn out just like him, obsessed with flying and airships—"

Joseph looked at the newspaper in her hand. "Oh Mum, I wasn't reading about— that. I was reading about... something else."

But it was too late, his mother was off on one of her extended recitations of all the things she was worried about, chief amongst them being that Joseph would take after his father, and be lost to her as well.

Usually he could let it wash over him, but today it just seemed too much to bear on top of all of his other worries. He suddenly decided he couldn't take it for another instant. Jumping up and running to the hall, he grabbed his coat and cap, and ran out of the front door.

It was a beautiful spring day, but Joseph saw none of it as he mooched along, head down, sad and worried. His route as always took him down from Newgate and past St Paul's. But as he turned into Cannon Street he noticed a flash of silver, seemingly just above Mansion House. An airship? He started to turn back to get a better look, then caught himself guiltily. Maybe his mother was right, he should just forget about airships.

But something about what he had seen nagged at him. Something unusual in the glimpse. His curiosity got the better of him, and he turned towards the Monument, and then walked down to and out onto London Bridge. He stopped suddenly, gripping the stone parapet, and stared downriver. The soft early morning light made the river golden, and Tower Bridge was just a silhouette. But above, and to the right, hanging motionless over the Isle of Dogs, was Aeropolis.

The floating city was a silver shimmer, catching a stronger light from the sun at its altitude. It seemed huge, much larger than Tower Bridge, and yet delicate and light, a fantasy of curved aluminium and silver-painted canvas. The haze of distance made its features slightly indistinct.

Despite his guilty misgivings Joseph had to admit it was an impressive sight. There was something otherworldly about it, floating above the workaday reality, and he could almost believe that the people who lived up there had escaped the mundane world that he inhabited, leaving behind all of its trouble and woe as they floated on high. He wondered what it would be like, to live like that.

As Joseph watched, a tiny silver speck of an airship rose from some hidden launchpad and made its way north, towards the City, gradually descending as it did so. The sight of it brought his dream to mind, and he saw again his father board just such an airship. He turned his back on it and strode doggedly off to work, head down.

Turning at the top of London Bridge Approach, he glanced backwards, and noticed that the ship seemed to be following him. Of course it wasn't really, but it did grow steadily larger, glinting in the sunlight, a hint of engine noise borne on the morning breeze. He turned into King William, and redoubled his pace, almost running towards the Bank of England. The ship moved smoothly overhead, its engines growing louder as it continued to descend. It appeared to be making for the landing pad on top of the Royal Exchange. There were markings on its tail fins, *H-1* in large lettering.

As the ship moved out of sight above the buildings, Joseph slowed to a walk and turned up an alleyway. Emerging into Lombard Street, he turned left and made for the entrance of the City & Empire Merchant Bank. He paused on its marble steps, wondering if it had in fact landed close by.

"Joey!" bawled a voice at his ear. He jumped and nearly fell into the street.

"Off in our dreamworld again, are we?" Mickey seemed to be able to make every syllable that he uttered to sound like a sneer. Joseph rolled his eyes and pushed past the older boy, footsteps echoing in the marbled entrance hall.

Mickey's voice continued regardless. "You'd better get up to the Chairman right quick, and no mistake! Been waitin' for you, 'ain't he?"

Joseph was confused. He wasn't late; in fact, having skipped breakfast, he was earlier than usual. The bank didn't open for business for an hour at least; as a messenger, and general office-boy, his first job was to see if there were any documents waiting to go out, but he knew there were no deals being closed at the moment, and hence no late-night drafting sessions: he didn't expect to find anything in his in tray. But maybe something had come up overnight. Joseph turned and ran up the marble staircase to Churchill's office, his heart thudding in his chest.

The door was open, and Churchill was standing next to his great mahogany desk, cigar in hand, as he looked out of the high window overlooking the Royal Exchange. Joseph crossed the Persian carpet again.

"Excuse me, sir?"

Churchill turned, and looked at Joseph. "Good morning, young man!" he boomed, smiling broadly. "What can I do for you?"

Joseph felt confused again. "Well, sir, Mickey said that you needed me, sir, and, well, I'm sorry I'm late..." he tailed off, not sure how to continue.

Churchill shook his great head. "You're not late, Joseph. I simply asked Cooper if he could have a messenger standing by, that's all." He moved to his upholstered leather chair, and sat down heavily. "I have an unscheduled meeting with an important client, and we may need to move quickly." He turned to his credenza, and lifted a crystal tumbler to his eye, as if contemplating the amber liquid it contained. "Yes, quickly indeed, is how Mr Howard Hughes likes to move..." he said, half to himself. But Joseph heard.

FIVE

There was a knock on the door. Joseph turned to see a slim man with slicked-back black hair and a neat moustache enter the room. He strode rapidly across the floor, radiating energy, and extended a hand.

"Mr Churchill. How are you doing?" He spoke with a strong American twang, his voice somewhat nasal. Churchill smiled broadly as his hand was seized and vigorously shaken.

"My dear Mr Hughes! How lovely to see you again."

Hughes paced around the room, glancing back at his entourage, who were only then catching up with him. He strode rapidly to the window, looked out at the view, and then turned back to face the room. "So are we meeting the investors here?"

Churchill looked taken aback. "Why, no! I had thought it best if we spoke a little about why you need funding first. I need to have an idea of the nature of the offering, so that I can choose the best investors to make my presentation to—"

"Ah, hell, Winston! That's gonna take ages!" Hughes grimaced impatiently. "Look, it's quite simple." He strode forward, his hands cutting through the air in decisive gestures. "The gusher of money I get from Tool Co is

21

running dry. Aeropolis is costing me an arm and a leg. The helium alone…" He shook his head. "I need money in Hughes Aircraft for a new project. A lot of money. And I'm prepared to sell shares in Aeropolis Holdings to get it."

Churchill nodded. "How many shares?"

"Not more than 20%. For 15 million."

Churchill nodded. "US dollars?"

Hughes looked at him scornfully. "Of course US dollars!" He suddenly stared directly at Joseph. "You boy!"

Joseph stiffened, feeling his cheeks redden. "Me, sir?"

"Yes you! Your collar is all skewiff. Straighten it please!" He continued to stare at Joseph, who felt his collar with nervous fingers, conscious that everyone in the room had their eyes on him. He straightened it as best he could, feeling embarrassed and angry.

"Much better." Hughes turned his attention back to Churchill. "So that's it. You better get on the horn to your investors."

Churchill blinked. "Well, I do need to know a bit more about the investment…"

Hughes sighed in a frustrated fashion. "It's Aeropolis, Winston! Everyone knows about her. We can go outside and look at her right now. But you've been on her before, right?"

Churchill shook his head. "No, I'm afraid I've not had the pleasure."

"What?" Hughes looked aghast. "Really? Well, let's go there now! I'll take you in my airship."

Churchill looked completely non-plussed. But Hughes was already heading for the door, herding his people out ahead of him. The Chairman made as if to follow, then turned to Joseph.

"Would you be so good as to find my briefcase and overcoat, and bring them down to the lobby for me?" And with that he was off after the departing Hughes.

Joseph grabbed the briefcase and coat, and made his way down the marble staircase. *So that was the great Howard Hughes? What an unpleasant man. I'm glad he's leaving so soon.*

He met the party in the lobby, putting on their coats and

getting ready to leave. As he made to hand the briefcase to Churchill, the Chairman turned to him, and smiled gently.

"Why don't you carry that for me, Joseph? And get your coat."

Joseph was taken aback. His first thought was that his mother would go ballistic if she knew he had travelled to Aeropolis. He opened his mouth to protest, but Churchill had already turned back to face Hughes. Joseph stood still for a moment, willing himself to tap Churchill on the shoulder and refuse the assignment. But something held him back. He was thinking about his conversation with Monmouth. *If I go along, maybe I can find out more about Hughes, satisfy myself as to whether there is anything to it. And if I do find anything suspicious, I can go straight to Monmouth.* He ran to find his coat, trying not to think about his mother. He buried the nagging feeling of guilt under a growing sense of excitement. *I'm going to Aeropolis!*

SIX

And so it was that Joseph found himself aboard Hughes's famous airship H-1. Feeling swept up by events, he had followed the group across to the Royal Exchange, into the large elevator, and up to the rooftop landing pad. The majestic airship sat in the centre, dominating the view. When Joseph had watched it flying in earlier, it had seemed small and sleek, but up close, it was imposingly large, the curve of the gas envelope looming out overhead, and blocking the early morning sun. The elegant gondola sat neatly under this bulk, like a bus under a whale. Once again, Joseph found himself guiltily admiring what he saw. He followed the others across the landing pad to the entry hatch. Pausing to run a hand in wonder over the lustrously shined wood of the doorframe, he caught himself irritatedly and hurried aboard.

Inside were dark wood panels, polished brass fittings and instruments, and soft burgundy leather seats. A pretty blonde stewardess welcomed him aboard, and directed him to his seat. As he sat down he noticed that Hughes had taken the right-hand command seat at the front of the cabin, where he was going through the pre-flight checklist with the co-pilot. *So Hughes flies his own airship, does he?* Joseph felt simultaneously impressed and annoyed by this.

After closing the door, the stewardess turned and took the seat next to him, buckling herself in with quick, efficient movements. Joseph immediately felt awkward as he fumbled with his own seatbelt. *I'm going to do something stupid, I just know I am.* The stewardess turned to help him, and he mumbled his thanks, feeling his cheeks burn.

"I'm Betty, by the way," said the stewardess in a soft American accent, turning on a dazzling smile. "I'm the stewardess on H-1."

Joseph's mouth went dry. *Why am I getting so nervous?* His brain seemed to be stuck as he looked down and away from her bright blue eyes. He forced himself to return her gaze. "I am Joseph Samson, and I work for Mr Churchill. At the bank. Do you live on Aeropolis? Well you must do, silly question really, how else could you always be available to work on H-1?" He became aware that he was speaking too quickly, and he stopped himself, blushing and dropping his gaze again.

When he looked back up again, Betty was smiling gently. "Well, you're right, I do live on Aeropolis. Will this be your first visit?"

Joseph smiled and nodded as she launched into a spirited description of what Aeropolis was like, but inwardly he was seized with the sudden fancy that she knew what Monmouth had asked him to do. It was a ridiculous thought, but he couldn't quite shake it. It must be because he felt guilty about his decision to spy on Hughes. *How do real spies stand it, pretending to be something they're not?*

The whine of starter motors drew Joseph's attention to the engine pod visible just forward of his porthole window, and he was hit with a sudden strong smell of aviation fuel as the engine roared into life, then throttled back to a rough idle. Joseph hadn't flown for more than a year, but the old familiar excitement came fluttering up inside him as Hughes motioned for the mooring lines to be released, and then swivelled the engine pods upwards with a practiced twist on the brass control levers. The agile ship fairly sprang off the deck, the roar of aero engines rising to a crescendo. As soon as they had cleared the roof structures, Hughes rotated the great engines forwards, and the ship accelerated into a sweeping, climbing turn that brought them up over the City and pointed towards Aeropolis.

Joseph's seat had an excellent view out of the forward-most port window. He didn't know what to look at first. From this new perspective on the City, the old stone seemed to glow in the soft golden light, the sky pale blue fading to peach. The imposing bulk of the Bank of England dwindled rapidly, and then the Monument came into view, the gilded flames on its top already below them. They slipped smoothly across the north bank of the Thames and over the great river itself. Joseph imagined that the ship must look like a silver rugby ball flying towards Tower Bridge, as if it were an immense set of goalposts. They cleared the crossbar easily.

Turning to look out of the front windscreen, his eye was caught by Aeropolis, gleaming silver in the clear morning light. He watched it grow rapidly larger as H-1's powerful engines closed the gap.

From below the main visible features were the two torus-shaped gas envelopes, one inside the other, that kept the vast city aloft. Betty pointed at them.

"Do you see those huge doughnut-shaped rings? Beneath the silver-painted fabric, there are great hoop-like girders of aluminium, holding immense gas cells. They contain more helium than exists in any other single structure anywhere on Earth."

Joseph turned to look at her in surprise. But Betty was oblivious, staring at the enormous structure with rapt fascination.

"Those giant buttresses, now. The huge holes in them save weight, you know." Joseph glanced at them, curving out from the girders. "But they're still strong enough to support the deck." Joseph supposed she meant the flat circular bit that sat on top of the toruses like a beer mat on a doughnut. He sighed and shook his head ruefully. As much as he tried not to be, he was fascinated and excited by what he was seeing.

"Do you get paid to talk about Aeropolis, like a tour guide?" he said, and then immediately felt bad. But Betty just smiled good-naturedly.

"I'm sorry if I seem a bit obsessed with Aeropolis. I guess I just love her so much!" She looked back at the object of her affection. Joseph felt slightly bemused by her attitude. And a tiny bit jealous, as well.

As H-1 gained altitude, more and more of the superstructure of the air city became visible above the great curved edge of the deck. First the central spike atop the control tower; and then the control tower itself, its panoramic windows facing out in all directions. Below the tower, the central structure of Aeropolis thickened and broadened, until at its base it took up about a third of the area of the main deck. As Betty continued her narration, he learned that it was composed of offices, private dwelling units, dormitories, barracks, bars, and restaurants. He could also see gun emplacements, communications arrays, balconies, promenades, viewing decks, and other structures whose purpose Joseph couldn't even begin to guess at.

At last H-1 rose above the level of the deck, bringing into view the landing pads, flight offices, and refuelling stations that occupied the rest of the main deck space. The circumference of the deck was punctuated with gun emplacements and rocket launchers. As they drew nearer, Joseph realised, with a thrill of fear, that some of the guns were tracking them. Hughes reached up for the microphone, contacting the tower for permission to approach and land. After a brief pause, permission and approach instructions were given, and the guns swivelled away.

But not aimlessly. By watching where they aimed, Joseph could see that they were tracking about a dozen other airships and aircraft converging on Aeropolis. There were ponderous freighters, zippy pleasure cruisers, and enormous passenger liners. All were moving purposefully towards one or another of the many landing pads.

Joseph's eye was suddenly caught by a small airship that was not following the pattern. As he stared out of his

27

window, he could see that the craft was not moving towards Aeropolis at all, but was instead heading directly towards H-1, and at high speed!

He tore his gaze away from the approaching airship, and touched Betty's arm. "What is that airship doing?"

She looked at Joseph slightly blankly, but when her gaze followed where Joseph's shaking hand was pointing, her demeanour changed instantly. "Mr Hughes, sir!" she shouted. "Incoming at nine o'clock!"

Hughes glanced to his left, and instantly put the airship into a steep dive. Joseph gasped as his stomach seemed to float up inside him, and he heard cries of alarm from Churchill and the others in Hughes's entourage. He turned to look out the window again: they had now descended below the level of the other airship, but it was still alarmingly close to them, and getting closer.

Joseph watched its nose, craning his head up as far as he could to follow it, until it moved beyond his field of view. He held his breath. Just as he started to think that the other airship had missed them, there was an impact which shook the entire airframe, followed by horrendous grinding and tearing noises — and then a high-pitched hissing sound, accompanied by periodic rapid flapping noises. "We're losing lift gas!" someone shouted, panic in his voice.

The nose of H-1 pitched forward in a steep dive, and Joseph had to grab on to his seat arms to stay upright as his stomach seemed to do a somersault from the sudden drop. Ahead he saw, through the windshield, the green hills of south London, growing larger at horrifying speed. H-1 was heading straight for the ground, and a certain crash!

SEVEN

Chaos ensued on the flight deck. Everyone seemed to be jumping up, or falling from their seats, and all the while shouting in fear and anxiety. Suddenly Churchill's voice boomed out, more loudly than Joseph had ever heard it.

"MY DEAR LADIES AND GENTLEMEN, I MUST INSIST THAT YOU RETURN TO YOUR SEATS AND BECOME QUIET!"

A sudden hush ensued, allowing Churchill to continue in a more moderate tone. "Please allow Mr Hughes to attempt to regain control of the airship, as that is our best and indeed only viable course of action at present."

Everyone turned to look at Hughes, who was a picture of absolute concentration as he struggled with the controls, sweat beading on his brow. He flipped switches and turned handles, issuing curt orders to the copilot, who was struggling with the engine controls. Suddenly the engines roared, and Joseph felt a weight pressing him into the seat cushions, as the airship pulled shudderingly out of its dive, and began to claw its way back into the sky.

Hughes relaxed somewhat, and reached again for the microphone.

"Mayday, Mayday, this is H-1. Sustained a collision on final approach. Aircraft damaged. Gonna try to carry on landing. Currently 2,000 feet below you and one mile north-west. Request airspace clearance, and emergency assistance standing by."

Once again the loudspeaker crackled into life. "H-1, this is Aeropolis Control. Status acknowledged. Attention all other aircraft: this is an emergency. Stand off from Aeropolis immediately and assume a holding pattern. No takeoffs are permitted until further notice. Emergency crews to full alert."

As H-1 strained upwards, engines roaring at maximum thrust to compensate for the lift gas lost in the collision, she found a rapidly emptying sky. But she was still climbing much too slowly.

Hughes turned to his copilot. "Emergency thrust, Mr Shepard."

"Aye aye sir," was the reply, and the copilot removed a limiting bar from the top of the throttle lever slots, allowing them to be pushed to the full extent of their travel. The engine sound rose to an even higher pitch, and thrumming vibrations shook the airframe.

"The engines won't last long on emergency power, but with luck we'll get home," said Betty, her expression grim. Joseph gripped his armrests even more tightly, willing the ship upwards.

Slowly, agonisingly slowly, H-1 clawed her way up to the level of Aeropolis, and at last the lowest levels of the superstructure were visible. Finally the landing pads on main deck came into view, and Hughes made directly for the nearest unoccupied one. As he throttled back the engines, the crippled airship collapsed onto the pad with a jarring impact, narrowly missing a decrepit-looking old airship, whose owner had run out to see what the commotion was about, and was then forced to scurry out of the way, his shabby leather coat flying as he ran. One of the engines died with a horrible screeching noise, as the others ground down into silence. Everyone sat in a stunned silence.

Joseph released his death grip on his armrests, as the relief began to flood into his mind. He laughed in delight. "We made it!"

"Thank God," said Betty, smiling broadly at him. Everyone else was smiling and laughing in relief. Everyone, that is, except Howard Hughes. With a face like thunder, he stalked to the hatch, opened it, and strode off across the landing pad without another word.

Betty and the rest of Hughes's entourage seemed to be left somewhat at a loss by this. After a moment of uncertainty, she bustled off, and the others gathered themselves together and began to exit the ship. Joseph looked across at Churchill, who shrugged.

As the euphoria of their survival faded, Joseph found himself thinking back to the moments before the collision. *Had the other pilots really been trying to hit them?* He bit his lower lip as he concentrated on remembering the scene.

"Are you all right, Joseph?"

Churchill was standing next to him, a look of concern on his face.

"Yes, sir." Joseph rose from his seat. "I'm fine."

"You seem preoccupied with something, though."

Joseph nodded. "I can't help but think that what we just went through was no accident."

"Really? Whatever do you mean?"

"Well, sir, the other airship was deliberately aiming to hit us! I saw it, through the porthole."

Just then Betty reappeared. She had recovered her smile, although it seemed ever so slightly forced now. "I'm so sorry about all this! I've managed to make contact with Blake Vanross, Mr Hughes's personal assistant. He will meet us in the Core. So if you'll follow me, I'll take you there now."

She led them out of the ship and across the landing pad to a small hut on its edge. It turned out to be sheltering the head of a flight of steel stairs that led below deck. At the bottom was a curved corridor, painted white and floored with metal grating. They followed it around until it came to a junction with a wide, straight corridor. Betty turned right and marched off down it, her heels echoing off the steel walls. Thick pipes ran along the upper parts of the walls and the ceiling, and bulkhead lights cast a harsh glow on the glossy painted surfaces.

The unfinished conversation with Churchill weighed on Joseph's mind as they made their way through a blur of corridors, stairs, companionways, and even moving walkways, making it hard for him to take it all in. Everywhere it seemed there was the clatter of feet on steel stair treads, whilst loud machinery thumped and hummed and whistled, clouds of steam issued from grates, and men in overalls moved about purposefully, for the most part ignoring the intruders. Finally they came to the base of a large open circular void, like a vertical tunnel, that stretched upwards hundreds of feet through what Joseph supposed must be the centre of the tower that made up the core of Aeropolis. Joseph stared up at the high curved surface. A number of bronze and glass lift gondolas were moving up and down vertical slots in the circular wall, and far above the brilliant gleam of bright sun illuminated a frosted skylight.

When Joseph looked down again, he saw a man approaching them across the wide floor of what must be the Core. The man was neatly dressed in a seersucker suit and bow tie, and he had a closely trimmed moustache. He nodded at Betty as he drew nearer, and then went to shake Churchill's hand.

"Mr Churchill. I am so sorry about your ordeal! Thank God you're OK. I'm Blake Vanross. Mr Hughes asked me to look after you while he is… engaged."

Churchill nodded. "Thank you, Mr Vanross. Might I enquire where Mr Hughes has gone?"

Vanross hesitated. "I can't be sure. But we can go to his office, perhaps you can wait there?"

"I'd very much care to be taken to Mr Hughes! I insist on knowing the truth about what has just occurred to put my own life, and that of my assistant, in jeopardy."

"As I've already said, Mr Churchill, I can't be sure where Mr Hughes is." Vanross's smile tightened. "As for the unfortunate occurrence on the airship, my information is that it was nothing more than a terrible accident. Now, if you'll just follow me to his office—"

"Mr Vanross." Churchill's voice overrode the other man's like a bull charging. "As *I* have already said, I have no intention of following you to anywhere other than where Mr Hughes is currently located. Furthermore, *my* information is that your so-called accident was nothing of the kind. I absolutely insist on being conducted to the presence of Mr Hughes so that he can explain why he has exposed us to deliberate attack. If you are unable to lead me in the desired direction, I must request that you find someone who can!"

As Churchill delivered himself of this speech, Vanross made vain attempts to interrupt, but by the end of it his face was pale and his mouth was set in a firm line as he stared at Churchill. The seconds ticked by as the two men stared at each other, unmoving.

EIGHT

The standoff continued, Vanross evidently trying to call Churchill's bluff. But the older man simply remained staring at him, an expectant look on his face. A sheen of sweat appeared on the brow of Vanross.

Then Betty stepped forward, smiling tightly. "I'm sure that Mr Hughes must have gone to the control room." She turned to Vanross. "What do you think, Blake?"

He glanced at her, narrowing his eyes, then dropped his gaze. His shoulders slumped. "Yes, I think that's right."

"Very good," said Churchill. "Would you like to take us to the control room, then?"

"Very well," Vanross said, bowing his head. "If you'll follow me, I'll take you to Mr Hughes." He led the way across the floor, his head held stiffly erect.

They walked across the round floor and through an archway in the far wall. By the time Joseph brought up the rear, Vanross was standing facing a set of closed sliding doors and inserting a key into a slot next to the doors. Seconds later they slid open, and the group hurried through them. Joseph saw that they were in one of the lift gondolas. The doors closed, and the lift zoomed upwards, making Joseph feel heavy on his feet.

Although he was at the back of the gondola, he was able to see over the heads of the others due to his height. Through the glass walls of the lift he could see the central core flash by. Below was the base, rapidly diminishing. The wall of the shaft was punctuated by windows, and he caught glimpses of each level as they passed. At first he saw machinery, pipes, tanks, and steel catwalks. Then came what looked like administrative levels, with plain carpeting and painted wood panels. As the elevator began to slow, Joseph saw more opulent levels, with plush carpeting or marble on the floors, and walls lined with flocked wallpaper or rich wood paneling.

At last the lift slowed to a stop, and the doors opened onto a functional-looking lobby walled in polished aluminium. Through the round portholes in double doors opposite the lift, Joseph glimpsed a dazzling vista of sky and cloud.

Vanross pushed through the doors, and the group followed him into a wide room that was flooded with light from curved glass outer walls. Joseph's eye was irresistibly drawn to the view through those immense windows. Below he could see the disc of Aeropolis' main deck, and beyond it, London lay resplendent in the mid-morning sun. Tower Bridge was clearly visible, while St Paul's dominated the City skyline. Further up the Thames lay the Houses of Parliament and Big Ben, and he thought he could even glimpse Buckingham Palace, next to the open green space of Hyde Park.

But Vanross continued to walk along the gallery that ran around the rear of the room, behind a row of curved desks. Each desk had a radio operator, equipped with headphones and a microphone, sitting in front of panels full of switches, dials and knobs. There was a constant low murmur of calm voices, and the distinctive smell of warm radio tubes.

It became obvious to Joseph as he followed Vanross that the control room encircled the entire top of the Core. After they had gone around nearly half way, they came upon a small group of men standing in the gallery. One of them was Howard Hughes. When he spotted them approaching, he detached himself from the group and walked over to meet them.

He scowled deeply at Vanross as he approached, and seemed about to say something to his assistant. But then he controlled himself with a visible effort, and turned to his guests. "I'm sorry you got caught up in this."

Churchill inclined his head slightly. "So am I. Although I am not entirely certain of what exactly I have been caught up in."

Hughes frowned at him. "Well, what does it look like? A simple accident, that's all."

"No, it wasn't!" The words were out of Joseph's mouth before he realised what he was doing. He felt the heat rising in his cheeks as Hughes turned to look at him.

"What are you talking about? Why would you say such a thing?"

Despite his antipathy towards the man, Joseph felt his will melt away in the face of the sheer power of Hughes's personality. His eyes seemed to lock on to Joseph's, his gaze demanding an answer.

Taking a deep breath, Joseph held the man's gaze as he replied. "I saw the pilots in the other ship. They were looking directly at us! It was no accident."

Hughes grimaced. "Ah, come on! Of course they were looking at us! They were trying to take evasive action!"

Joseph shook his head, grim determination filling him. He might have gotten into this without thinking, but now that he had, he wasn't going to be fobbed off. "No sir, that's not right. When you put H-1 into a dive, they went nose-down as well." Joseph moved his hands to show how the other ship had followed H-1's movements. "They were deliberately trying to hit us!"

Hughes bounced on his toes and clenched and unclenched his fists, agitation adding to his nervous energy. "Are you absolutely sure of this?"

"Yes, sir."

Hughes held his gaze for a long moment, but Joseph did not flinch. Finally Hughes looked away, grimacing and biting his lip. Joseph felt as if a searchlight had been turned away from him. He let out his breath slowly.

Another member of the other group, a tall and well-built blond man, detached himself and strode rapidly over to join them. He was wearing a leather flying jacket and a peaked cap with gold wings on the front. He had a very stern expression on his face.

"What's happening, Clive?" said Hughes. The blond man nodded in greeting to Churchill. "Clive Thornton, commander of the Air Corps, Mr Churchill. Pleased to meet you," he said, although he didn't look as if he were ever pleased with anything.

He turned back to Hughes. "Johnson has just rendezvoused with the ship. It seems to be drifting and unmanned."

"Unmanned? Impossible!"

A flicker of irritation passed over Thornton's face. "Johnson saw two parachutes far below, when he first spotted the ship. We think they bailed out."

Hughes glanced at Joseph. "But the ship was completely airworthy."

Thornton nodded. "Well, yes. No damage severe enough to keep her from flying."

Hughes nodded, frowning deeply. "So if they jumped out, it was because they didn't want to be around when we caught up with the ship. Did Johnson send anyone after the 'chutes?"

"He did. McRae is doing a sweep of the countryside below. But it's heavily wooded. Even if he finds the 'chutes, they'll probably be able to sneak away without being seen."

Hughes bit his lower lip, obviously agitated. "I don't care, they've got to keep on it."

"Oh, they will."

Hughes moved slightly closer to Thornton, and spoke again in a lower voice. Joseph had to strain to hear what he said. "Any sign of Zee A involvement?"

Thornton's reply was soft as well. "It's impossible to say for sure. The ship is a standard freighter, fairly old, crudely modified with an iron I-beam bolted to the underside of the gondola to act as a battering ram. We're running checks on her ownership history now."

"Good. Let me know what you find out."

"Of course, sir." With a nod, Thornton returned to his group, and began an urgent conversation in low tones.

Hughes turned to his guests. "Well, it sure looks as if I owe young Joseph here an apology." He looked away for a few moments, grimacing and rubbing his jaw, and clenching his fists. He was such a bundle of suppressed energy that Joseph half expected him to start bouncing off the walls. Then he took a deep breath, stood up straighter, and turned back to face Churchill again.

"Anyway, I guess there's nothing we can do about it now. As soon as I hear anything from Thornton, I'll let you know. In the meantime, we should get back to what we had originally planned to do. Come to my offices." He strode off towards the lifts without a backward glance, and Joseph and Churchill hurried after him.

This time the journey was short. Hughes's offices were only one floor down, and the view from the window was just as breathtaking as that from Control. Better, in fact, as there were no desks in the way, and Joseph was able to go right up to the window in the reception area.

Hughes joined him. "Aren't you afraid of the height?" He looked at Joseph skeptically.

Despite his determination not to like Hughes, Joseph found himself admiring the aviator's directness. At least one knew where one stood with Hughes. "No sir, I love the view!"

Hughes raised an eyebrow, and nodded approvingly. "So do I." He turned and walked rapidly back to where Churchill was standing in front of the receptionist's desk. Joseph followed him, silently berating himself for falling under Hughes's spell. *Don't forget how rude he was to you in Churchill's office!* He resolved to be on his guard.

Churchill was speaking to the receptionist. "Could you look after my assistant Joseph while I meet with Mr Hughes?"

The receptionist turned to look at Joseph, a smile on her face. She had pretty auburn hair and green eyes. Hughes seemed to surround himself with attractive women. Nervous butterflies immediately filled his stomach. He always got so tongue-tied when he received attention from a pretty girl.

But before she could reply, Hughes interrupted. "Let the boy join us, Winston. Dawn has enough work to do without having to babysit him." He turned and strode into his office, leaving Joseph silently seething. *Babysit me? What does he think I'll do?*

Churchill looked doubtful. "Well, I suppose you could sit in. But Joseph, you must never speak to anyone about what is discussed in this office. Do you understand? It is very important that the bank's clients have complete trust in our discretion."

Joseph should have been happy at his reprieve, but instead felt a stab of disappointment. "I understand, sir, but really, I'd be quite happy to stay out here—"

"No, on reflection, it will be good for your education. Besides, if Mr Hughes has requested that you join us, it's best that we respect his wishes as a client."

And so, with a last confused glance at the receptionist, who gave a rueful shrug, he followed Churchill into Hughes's private office, and closed the doors behind them.

NINE

Hughes was pacing up and down behind his desk. "Come on, Winston! Look around you!" He raised his arms in big sweeping gestures, taking in their surroundings. "You're sitting in an office at the top of a tower that is *floating in mid-air!* I've created something incredible here. The technological challenges that we've overcome to build Aeropolis are nothing short of staggering. This is the most amazing machine that has ever been built, the pinnacle of the technological age." He stared at Churchill. "This is the investment opportunity of a lifetime! Who wouldn't want to be part of it?"

Churchill seemed unmoved by this. "Oh, there is no doubt that you have a fine technological achievement. But Howard, what exactly is it that Aeropolis is for? How do you make money?"

Joseph was quite taken aback by this. He hadn't ever given a thought to what Aeropolis was *for.* The fact that she existed at all was more than enough for him to take in. But thinking about it, he supposed that there would have to be some sort of economic basis for that existence: even Hughes could not have enough money to have built her purely for the pleasure of doing so.

He turned his attention back to Hughes, who had became even more agitated. "What is she for?" He rolled his eyes, seemingly exasperated beyond measure. "She is a floating free port, a place anyone can come to buy or sell or transship cargo of any description!"

"Why on Earth should anyone want to bring their cargo all the way up here?" rumbled Churchill, nipping the end off of a cigar as he did so.

Again Joseph found himself surprised by Churchill's question. He turned eagerly to see what the reply would be. But Hughes seemed to abruptly run out of steam. He flopped into his chair, and spoke in a quiet, almost resigned tone.

"They do it to save money, Winston. There are no tariffs and no taxes up here."

"Well then, how do you expect to make the money to pay the dividend?" came the instant reply. Joseph grinned; he was enjoying this. *Wriggle out of that!*

Hughes took a deep breath, sat up a bit straighter, and smoothed down his jacket lapels with his thumbs. "OK, so here's how that works." His voice took on a didactic tone. "When a shipping company uses a normal, ground-based port, they pay tariffs and taxes to the government, not to the base operator, and they don't get any real benefit in return for those payments. They've also got to pay landing fees, rental on office and warehouse space, and so forth, to the base operator.

"So when they come to Aeropolis, they're making savings on the tariffs and taxes, but they're not going to expect to get the real services for free! They're happy to pay rent, landing fees, all the rest. We also levy a flotation charge, which the carriers can only avoid if they bring us fuel and helium. We make a small turn on the charge."

Churchill applied a lighter flame to the end of his cigar, and puffed it into life. "Are you getting any Zeppelins calling?"

A flicker of annoyance passed over Hughes's face. "No,

we're still working on that."

"I've heard that Herr Doktor Eckener is not your greatest fan." Churchill blew a perfect smoke ring towards the ceiling.

Joseph smirked. The antipathy of the head of the Zeppelin company for Hughes was well known. It had all started when Eckener had tried to sell airships to the US Navy. Hughes had won the contract instead, and Hugo Eckener was by all accounts a remarkably poor loser.

But Hughes seemed unfazed. "He'll see reason in time. We could save them a small fortune in tariffs."

"What other sources of income do you have?"

Hughes rolled his eyes, but kept his tone measured. "We also rent out office space to international companies, and we've got some great luxury apartments, with very steep rents, which have become the latest thing amongst the rich. And then there's the hotel and casino."

"Harrumph. It still sounds decidedly precarious to me," said the Chairman. But there was a faint smile on his lips.

Joseph felt that he was starting to understand what was going on. It was a kind of game played between the two of them, with Churchill pretending to be the skeptical investor, teaching Hughes that while the merits of an investment in Aeropolis might be obvious to him, he still needed to make the effort to explain them in detail. Joseph himself had no idea how the investors would react, but he did have to admit that Hughes seemed well in command of the facts. He had simply assumed that Aeropolis was Hughes's folly, the quixotic idea of a man with more money than sense. There did seem to be a bit more to it than that.

The meeting turned towards more detailed matters. Hughes unfolded a series of sheets of paper, all covered with figures, and Churchill pointed to first this one, then that one, peppering Hughes with questions and observations about the financial health of Aeropolis. Most were answered easily enough, but Hughes deferred some of them for further analysis by his chief accountant.

Joseph had enjoyed the initial interaction between the two men, but this was just boring. His thoughts turned back to his meeting with Monmouth. He looked at Hughes, engrossed in the numbers, and tried to decide if it was possible that this man could be responsible for the death of his father. Despite his eccentricities, Hughes looked much more like a sober businessman than a crazed murderer. But then appearances could be deceptive. *I'll need to find out more. Keep my eyes and ears open, maybe sneak a look at some files.* The thought of being a spy was thrilling and scary at the same time. He felt a fluttering sensation in his stomach.

Suddenly the door opened, and a young girl dashed into the room. She was about Joseph's age, and red-haired with big green eyes. She ran across the plush carpet, and threw her arms around Hughes's neck.

"Daddy! Oh, I heard about the crash! I was so worried! Are you all right?"

Hughes hugged his daughter to him, smiling indulgently. "Of course I am, angel. Nothing's going to happen to me!" He patted her back affectionately.

"I guess I'd better introduce you to our guests." He gently released his embrace, and the girl turned, slightly shyly, to face them. "This young tearaway is my daughter, Ione."

Churchill inclined his head graciously. "I am very pleased to make your acquaintance, Miss Hughes. I am Winston Churchill, and this is my assistant, Joseph Samson."

Ione Hughes seemed to recover her poise, and walked slowly over to them. "Pleased to meet you, Mr Churchill," she said, holding out her hand, which Churchill was obliged to shake. Then she turned to Joseph. The demure smile was replaced by a far more appraising look. Joseph felt that he was being minutely inspected, and he wasn't sure that he measured up.

"Hello, Joseph. Your first time on Aeropolis? You don't look like you belong here, to be quite honest," she said.

Joseph was taken aback by this, and didn't have the faintest idea of how to respond. He thought she was very pretty, which only made her rudeness harder to take. Fortunately Churchill came to his rescue. "Joseph works with me in my bank. He's here to assist me."

Ione gave Joseph a cool nod, then turned back to her father. "Daddy, it's time for lunch! You promised we could go to Top Table!"

Hughes grimaced. "Ah, gosh, the, um, accident this morning has thrown my schedule totally off track. Mr Churchill and I are going to work through lunch to catch up: I've got a board meeting this afternoon that I can't reschedule."

Ione looked thoroughly deflated. "But you promised!" she pouted.

Hughes looked distressed. Then suddenly his face lit up. "I know! Why don't you go for lunch with young Joseph here?"

Ione's pout softened ever so slightly. "Can we still go to Top Table?"

"Sure, absolutely," said Hughes, somewhat distractedly. He was already engrossed in the papers on his desk.

"Come on then," said Ione with a sigh of resignation, not even looking at Joseph. She turned and skipped out of the door. As Joseph made to follow her, Hughes called him back.

"Oh, Joseph, hold on a sec, let me give you one of these." He was scribbling on a small card with a silver fountain pen. "This'll let you charge the meal to my account." He handed it over. Joseph grabbed it, anxious to hurry after Ione, and stuffed it into a pocket of his jacket. He nodded his thanks, and dashed out of the door.

TEN

Top Table was on the same floor as Hughes's office, and Joseph caught up with Ione after a few moments. She was standing just inside the entrance to the restaurant, speaking with a little man. He was immaculately dressed in a white formal jacket and bow-tie, with slicked-back hair and a very thin moustache.

As Joseph approached, the man turned to look at Joseph, rather disapprovingly. "Pardonne, monsieur, but ze restaurant is fully booked for lunch today."

Ione let out a peal of laughter. "Oh, Pierre, this is my guest, Mr Joseph Samson. It's just the two of us, Father can't make it for lunch today."

Pierre nodded briskly. "Of course. If monsieur and mademoiselle would be so kind as to follow me..." Turning away with a sort of bowing, sweeping motion, he walked off. Ione followed immediately, and Joseph hurried to remain by her side.

As he walked he barely noticed the sumptuous restaurant, with its thick, soft carpets, delicate gold-patterned wallpaper, and crystal chandeliers; he was too busy worrying about what he was going to talk about with this strange girl for an entire lunch. Part of him still seethed at the way she had treated him when they met; but another part was intrigued by her confidence. *And also by how pretty she is.* The admission made his cheeks burn.

The restaurant was completely full of well-dressed folk, talking and laughing quietly, or enjoying the food; but he felt quite a few curious eyes on him, as the maitre d' led them through the very centre, right up to a table in prime position, next to the central window that looked out over the main deck of Aeropolis far below.

Pierre snapped his fingers as they approached, and two waiters materialised: at a hand signal they rapidly and silently removed two of the place settings. Ione was seated at one of the remaining two by Pierre, whilst Joseph seated himself at the other, opposite Ione. After handing menus to them both, with an ingratiating bow to Ione, and a slightly disapproving glance at Joseph, Pierre was gone.

The magnificent view beckoned, but Joseph was distracted by the thought that he was out of place here. Although his mother tried to make sure that his clothes were neat and in good repair, there was no doubt that she favoured clothes that were durable and hard-wearing rather than fashionable. Joseph looked at the silk suits and beautiful poplin shirts worn by the men around him, and then at his own sturdy brown woollen jacket and grey flannel trousers. His shirt was clean, but the cuffs were not French ones. They had buttons instead of cufflinks, and they were slightly frayed. He tried to pull his jacket sleeves down over them.

The other distraction was the menu. It was in French, a language with which Joseph had a difficult, even tempestuous, relationship. At that moment he found himself unable to understand what at least half of the items were. And the prices! He was very glad that Hughes had given him the charge card: he didn't have enough money in his pockets to pay for even the cheapest item. Feeling more and more out of place, Joseph looked miserably across at his dining companion, who seemed to be in her element. She was pointing at something through the window.

"Oh, look! Is that Buckingham Palace?"

Her pronunciation of the final syllable annoyed him. *There's no ham in Buckingham!* "Yes, I do believe it is Buckingham Palace," he said, slightly emphasising the correct pronunciation. But Ione seemed not to notice, staring at the palace with an excited expression on her face.

If Joseph had been shown a photograph of Ione, he would probably not have called her beautiful. But in person she was so lively and vivacious that it was impossible not to think of her as attractive. She was certainly striking, with flaming red hair, prominent cheekbones, and a strong jawline, just like her mother, the famous Katherine Hepburn.

Despite this, he found himself resenting her. Or perhaps he only resented the idea that he should automatically fawn over her because she was the daughter of a rich and powerful man and a famous movie star. He became determined not to do so.

"Have you ever been there?' she asked, turning her intense gaze to focus on him.

"Er, no." He frowned, feeling awkward. "Only lords and ladies and earls and so forth are invited to the Palace."

Ione nodded. "I suppose it's a bit like the White House. Where the President is, in Washington DC." She smiled. "Daddy's been there, of course."

Oh, of course. Why would the President deny himself the counsel of the great Howard Hughes? Her direct way of speaking suddenly reminded him of how her father had spoken to him in Churchill's office. "Was he rude to the President as well?"

Ione looked quite taken aback. "What do you mean?"

Joseph immediately regretted his impulsive comment. "Nothing." He cleared his throat, sitting up straighter, and pretended to concentrate on the menu. "Have you decided what you'd like to order yet?"

But Ione was having none of it. When he glanced up he found that she was still staring intently at him. "What did you mean by that comment, Joseph?"

"Nothing. I'm sorry. I shouldn't have said it."

She stared at him for a few moments more, then nodded,

and looked down at her own menu. He felt relieved, and then irritated that he felt relieved. *Why should I be intimidated by you?* He cleared his throat again. "In Mr Churchill's office this morning," he began, then faltered when Ione's eyes flicked up like searchlights. He frowned, and pressed on doggedly. "Well, your father, he told me to straighten my collar. Not in a nice way. I just found it to be rude." He tailed off, and sat there feeling apprehensive. *Now I'm going to get it.*

But instead of responding, Ione dropped her eyes to her lap, looking upset. Joseph immediately felt guilty. When she spoke, it was in a quiet voice that he had to strain to hear.

"I know what you mean. He sometimes does that to people. I don't know why. Tells them to straighten their clothing, or clean a speck of dust. It's very embarrassing."

Joseph was feeling embarrassed himself. This certainly wasn't what he had expected would happen. "It's all right," he said. "No harm done."

Ione looked at him sadly. "It's not all right, not really." Her face became earnest. "He's a good person. I want you to know that. He wasn't trying to hurt you." She shook her head. "It's like something takes him over, he can't stop himself."

Joseph didn't know what to say to that. The silence lengthened, and was broken only when Pierre arrived to take their order.

"The usual for me, Pierre," said Ione. He nodded, and turned to Joseph, a smirk on his face. Joseph pointed out what he hoped was onion soup and some sort of stew, not even attempting to pronounce the names, which seemed to take the wind out of Pierre's sails somewhat. He flounced off, leaving Joseph dreading the resumption of the silence.

But Ione seemed to have recovered herself, and she launched into a detailed reminiscence of a trip to Kensington Gardens with her mother.

"We went to see the statue of Peter Pan. Didn't you just love that story when you were a child?"

"Peter Pan? Wasn't he the boy who refused to grow up?"

"Yes!" Her eyes shone. "And he flew away to Never-Never

Land! I always wanted to do that. I used to leave my window open at night, hoping he would come and get me."

Joseph snorted. "Aren't you a bit old for that sort of thing?"

Ione narrowed her eyes at him. "I didn't say I did that now! It's just a treasured memory from childhood. Surely you can understand that?"

"Not really, no. When I was a child I believed... well, all sorts of stupid things. But I'm not a child anymore. I know that dreams don't come true, and that the best thing you can do is accept the reality."

"What reality is that, Joseph?"

He felt the anger flare inside him, like a match lighting a fuse. He tried to control it, but the words came out hard and bitter. "The reality of life! That it's hard, and horrible, and the people you rely on let you down!"

Ione stared at him, shocked. "Oh Joseph, I'm so sorry that you feel that way."

For some reason her concern made him even more angry. The red tide carried him on, and he let it rise. "I don't need you to feel sorry for me!" He glared at her. "Anyway, you needn't act as if you're superior to me. My father may have abandoned me, but your father is crazy. You admitted as much a few moments ago!"

No sooner were the words out of his mouth than Joseph realised he had gone too far. Ione stared at him, speechless for a moment. Then her face crumpled. "How could you say that? He's not crazy! He's a good man, I told you that!" Her lower lip quivered, and then came the first sob.

Joseph felt mortified. He hadn't meant to make her cry, but his anger had gotten the better of him. "Ione, I'm sorry, I didn't mean it!" People at surrounding tables were turning to look at them. He jumped up from his seat and rushed around to her side of the table, holding out his napkin like a sacrificial offering.

"Don't touch me!" Ione shrank away from him, then stood up, and ran from the restaurant, sobbing.

Conversation at the tables around Joseph had ceased, and

it felt as if everyone in the restaurant were staring at him. He felt sick, wanting to run after her, but knowing it would only increase his humiliation. He wished he were somewhere else, anywhere but there. He looked around at the staring mass, and for an instant he had a mad fancy to burst through the window of the restaurant and fly free of the pressure of their gaze. Closing his eyes, he took a deep breath to calm himself. Then, with burning cheeks, he forced himself to rise slowly and march out of the restaurant with as much dignity as he could muster, conversation slowly resuming in his wake. At every moment he fought the urge to break into a run. He concentrated on putting one foot in front of the other at a steady pace, and at last he reached the door, and the derisive smirk of Pierre.

Outside the restaurant he paused, not knowing what to do. Churchill and Hughes did not expect him to return for an hour at least, and he felt nervous about encountering the magnate again: what if he were really angry about how Joseph had spoken to his daughter? What if he asked Churchill to give Joseph the boot? What if she was in there now, demanding that action be taken?

He shrugged defiantly. So what if she was? Why should he care what any of them thought? He wasn't even supposed to be here. If Churchill hadn't dragged him along, none of this would have happened.

Still, as long as I'm here, I might as well take a look around. What with everything that had happened since boarding the airship, he had almost forgotten about spying on Hughes. But now that he was alone, and not expected to be anywhere in particular, it occurred to him that it was a golden opportunity to see what he could find out about Hughes's little world. He strode to the lift bank with determination, and pressed the button to descend.

ELEVEN

The lift reached the bottom of the Core, and Joseph emerged, some of his determination having evaporated on the ride down. He looked uncertainly at the corridors leading off the circular floor, trying to decide which one he had come down when he had arrived, but they all looked the same. He supposed that it didn't really matter which one he took, as he wasn't trying to get back to H-1 in any event. He had a vague plan of getting onto the main deck, and trying to talk to some of the aircrew. He thought that as long as he steered clear of the Core, no-one would recognise him. He picked a corridor entrance at random, and set off.

It rapidly became clear that he had not chosen well. Instead of the relatively wide and straight corridors that Betty had led them through, he found himself in a maze-like warren of short, tight companionways interspersed with larger spaces that were filled with hissing, clanking machinery and pipes. It seemed he had stumbled into some sort of engineering area, and there was no obvious route through it. He decided to return to the Core and try a different corridor.

But retracing his steps was more easily thought of than

carried out. He couldn't remember all of the twists and turns that he had taken, and after half an hour of traipsing up and down the narrow corridors, the noise of the machines making it hard to think, he had to admit that he was lost.

He had passed two or three boiler-suited engineers during his travels, who bustled past him with scarcely a glance, but now there was no-one to be seen. He tried to fight down a rising sense of panic as he walked, with ever-increasing pace, around corner after corner, never seeing anything but another short corridor. Just before he actually started running, he forced himself to stop, and take calming breaths.

There must be a way out of this maze. He carried on breathing deeply, and looked slowly around him. Up until that point he had not paid much attention to any of the corridors themselves, being focused only on where they would lead to. But now he noticed that there was a door on the left hand side of the one he was in, with a small round window in it. He peered through the wired glass, and saw steps leading downwards. Pushing the door open, he descended the steps.

On the next level, the little window in the door leading out of the stairwell showed a great bustle of people moving past it. He emerged into a wide and very busy thoroughfare. As he stared at the passing crowd, he was bumped by a short fat man in a chef's uniform. The man glared at him in irritation, and Joseph stepped back against the wall, only to block the progress of a thin-faced woman in a business suit. She pushed past him, shaking her head. Joseph shrank against the wall, feeling bewildered. He would need to get going if he was to avoid being a permanent roadblock. But which way should he go?

After a moment, it came to him. If Aeropolis was a floating city, these narrow corridors were her streets, or at least some of her streets. When he was trying to find his way in a city, he used street names, and sometimes signs with arrows pointing towards things, such as the signs in the City pointing towards St Paul's, or the Tower.

On the wall opposite, above the heads of the throng, he could actually see some sort of sign. He turned cautiously, looking up, and saw the same thing painted on the wall above his head. Unfortunately he couldn't make much sense of it. There were letters, and numbers, and arrows, but it might as well have been in a foreign language for all the meaning it conveyed to him. Joseph's shoulders slumped, the panic rising again. He felt trapped in the warren of tunnels. *I have to get out!*

He fought the panic down with an effort, trying to think calmly and logically. Obviously this part of Aeropolis was not exactly like a city; it was more like a very large ship. The people who lived and worked on it must use these coded signs so that they could find their way precisely. Vague directions like "this way to the main deck" would be pretty useless; the deck was huge. You would need to find your way to a particular part of it for the signs to be useful.

He was going to have to ask someone. He looked at the busy faces bustling past him, and quailed. They all looked so purposeful, striding rapidly along. Would they even stop to hear his request? But the only alternative was to wander around here until he somehow stumbled across either the Core or the main deck access. Given the size of Aeropolis, that wasn't an option. He steeled himself, and started to look for a likely target.

He tried to catch the eye of a bowler-hatted man hurrying past, but the man looked right through him, and continued going. Turning away, he saw a middle-aged woman with a formidable handbag, walking more slowly. He walked right up to her, but again, she brushed smoothly past him with a murmured pardon.

Joseph began to despair. *Some spy I'm turning out to be.* He imagined wandering around for hours, while Churchill wondered what had happened to him. Probably he would have Hughes mount a search! The idea of being found and rescued, like a lost child, just didn't bear thinking about. *I can't let that happen!*

He took a deep breath, drew himself up to his full height, threw his shoulders back, and marched quickly to intercept the nearest man.

"Excuse me, sir," he said, very loudly, laying a hand on the man's forearm. The man stopped, and turned to Joseph. "Can I help you, young sir?" he said, not unkindly, but in a slightly weary way. He was wearing faded but clean overalls, and a flat cap. He had a bushy moustache.

Joseph took a deep breath. No point being embarrassed now. "I'm lost, sir. I've been trying to find my way by looking at those codes, but I don't understand them." He pointed at the nearest sign.

The man chuckled. "Not surprising. The codes are gibberish if you don't know what they mean!" Then he frowned. "Why do you think that they tell you where to go?"

Joseph flushed. "I just presumed that they were like signposts in a normal city, only coded."

"Well, they do tell you where you are," the man said, nodding, "and if you know how Aeropolis is laid out, and how the codes work, you can use them to navigate. Where are you trying to get to?"

Joseph thought for a second. The sensible thing would be to just get directions back to the Core. But if this man helped him find his way, then he wouldn't have to go scuttling back to Hughes's office, defeated. He would still be able to carry out his mission. "I'm trying to get out onto the main deck."

"But where on the main deck?"

"Doesn't matter, really, I just want to get to the airships."

The man smiled. "Ah, an airship spotter, are we?" He walked over to the sign that Joseph had pointed at. It read "WX-2-1—>." He reached up and touched the letters. "Don't worry about these: they tell you which quadrant you're in. What you need to concentrate on are the numbers." He moved his finger to the first number. "This one, the zone number, tells you how far out from the Core you are: the higher the number, the further out. To get to the main deck you need to be on at least 5 before you start to go up, otherwise you'll come out in one of the central structures. Got that?"

Joseph nodded. "Yes, sir. What does the other number mean?"

The man frowned slightly. "Was just coming to that. It's a depth marker. Aeropolis goes down fifteen decks below the main deck, which is deck zero. Deck one is just below main deck, and so on."

"So in order to get out to main deck, I just need to follow the corridor out until I get to the fifth zone, and then I go up one deck?"

The man was positively beaming. "Exactly!"

"But which way do I go? Which way is out, and which way is in?" asked Joseph, hoping that the answer wouldn't be to go to the next junction and see if the zone number was higher, or lower.

"Ah, now that's where the arrow comes in," said the man. "The arrow points towards the Core. So to get to a higher zone number, go in the opposite direction."

"Thank you very much," said Joseph. The man smiled again. "No problem at all." And with that he was off.

Turning back to the coded sign, Joseph was careful to move off in the opposite direction to the arrow. At the next junction, he anxiously scanned the sign. It read "WX-3-1—>," with the arrow pointing in the direction he had come from. So he had successfully moved into the third zone! It was working the way the man had said.

Joseph hurried on, first into zone four and then into zone 5. According to what the man had told him, this should have meant he could now ascend to main deck. But where were the stairs going up? None of the doors in this section of the corridor had the little round windows in them. He tried a few of the doors, but they were mostly locked. One opened onto a huge echoing space which was in half-darkness, while others were doors to supply cupboards or storerooms.

He walked on a little further, but the little round windows remained elusive. He kept walking, fighting a growing sense of unease, moving into zone six, then into zone seven. There was still no sign of any means of ascent to the next deck, and just when he had come to terms with the idea of asking for help again, the stream of people, which had been steadily declining, dried up altogether.

Joseph stopped, wondering whether to turn back and find someone to ask, or press on regardless, despite his growing feeling that he was headed in the complete wrong direction. He squinted and peered ahead up the corridor, and saw what looked like daylight, streaming into the end of the tunnel. He decided to see what it was.

TWELVE

For some time the light seemed to get no closer, just brighter. Suddenly the corridor ended on a balcony or walkway that encircled a large void, which was open to the sky above; this was where the light was coming from. Joseph walked out onto the balcony, and peered over the railing at its edge. He could see into a shaft, easily thirty feet across, that disappeared down into the bowels of Aeropolis. The edges of the decks below made concentric circles that narrowed into gloom, where he could just make out rhythmic movement. A deep, throbbing bass note rose from the depths.

As Joseph peered downwards, trying to make out what he was seeing, the sound began to increase in pitch, and the movements seemed to speed up as well. A slight breeze touched Joseph's face, blowing from below. It quickly grew stronger, until his hair was blown backwards from his face, and yet it continued strengthening. Eventually he had to step back out of the blast of air, as his eyes were watering from the strength of the airflow. He realised that there must be a giant fan at the bottom of the shaft, but whether it was for ventilation or height regulation he couldn't have said.

Movement on the next deck down caught his eye. A small group of young men, dressed in greasy overalls and with blackened hands and faces, were gathering at the lower rail. Suddenly, with a loud whoop, one of them climbed up over the railing and launched himself into the howling gale. He spread his arms and legs out from his body, slightly bent, and was instantly caught by the airflow, which lifted him up into the air.

As he rose above Joseph's level, he pulled his arms and legs in a little, which caused him to stop rising, and then to ever so slowly drop downwards. With small hand movements he rotated himself so that he was facing his mates, and then he drifted slowly towards them. They were cheering and hooting, laughing and shouting above the din of the airflow, and two of them climbed up on the railing and hauled him in as he drifted into range.

No sooner had he touched down, to great acclamation and slaps on the back from the group, than a second young man, larger and heavier than the first, launched himself into the airstream. He was much less skilled, falling nearly all the way to the next level before managing to position himself into the configuration for ascending, and even then, his movements were jerky, and his progress was anything but smooth. As he rose over the edge of the railing, his eyes met Joseph's, and there was instant animosity in his gaze.

He floated slowly, in fits and starts, over to the railing in front of Joseph, and seized it as Joseph stepped back. Then he proceeded to haul himself over the railing, managing to gain his footing without falling over, although his movements were nowhere near as graceful as those of the first lad.

Straightening up slowly, upper lip curled in a sneer, he called over his shoulder. "Hey boys, lookee what we got up here!"

There was a clattering and a clanging on a stairwell, and in seconds the whole gang was pouring out of a corridor to the left of Joseph, and forming a loose circle around him. They stood, arms folded, staring at him, some with curiosity, others with animosity. Joseph looked apprehensively from face to face, trying to find someone with a friendly expression. But no-one was smiling. The howl of the airflow in the shaft suddenly diminished, and then fell away to silence.

"Who are you, boy? And why are you trespassing on 'prentice deck?" demanded the heavyset lad.

Joseph felt his anger rising, despite the implicit threat of the gang. "I'm not trespassing on your stupid deck! If anything I'm trying to find a way to get off of it!"

There were murmurs of anger at this. The other boy turned to the crowd. "Stupid deck, is it?" He turned back to Joseph. "Maybe it is, but it's *our* deck, matey. And we don't take kindly to people trespassin' and making disparagin' comments about her." He looked around his audience, a smirk on his face. "Especially not beanpoles."

The murmurs increased and turned to jeering. Joseph felt a stab of fear from the growing hostility. He hadn't done himself any favours with his angry outburst. These boys obviously considered it their home, and would defend it against an outsider. He decided to try a more conciliatory approach.

"Look, I just want to find my way onto main deck. I don't want any trouble!"

The heavyset boy stepped forward. "Well, you might not want trouble," he said in a low and menacing voice, "but you've definitely got some." He balled his right hand into a fist, and slammed it into his open left palm. The impact made a loud slapping sound in the silence. He took another step towards Joseph.

As he did so, a lad broke out of the circle to Joseph's left, and stepped in front of the heavyset boy. Joseph recognised him as the first boy he had seen flying in the airflow, the graceful one.

"Leave him alone, Mo. He's done nothing wrong," said the other boy. He was taller than Mo, and fair, but much more wiry. Mo glared at him. "Stay out of this, Harry. It doesn't concern you."

"Actually it does. If you get caught beating up another toff, we'll all be in for punishment duty," replied Harry firmly, meeting Mo's gaze. A murmur of dissatisfaction made its way through the circle around the three boys. Mo tried to stare Harry down, but the latter stood his ground.

Finally Mo took a step back, throwing his arms up and smiling. "Come on, mate! Can't you take a joke?" He forced a laugh. Harry relaxed, and grinned slightly, uncertainly. Mo moved towards him, the grin cracking his face, but not touching his eyes, which glared still. Joseph felt he should warn Harry, but it was too late: Mo pretended to put his arm across Harry's shoulders, but instead, in one smooth movement, hooked a foot behind Harry's heels, and pushed him in the chest with his other arm. Harry fell flat on his back onto the deck, all the air leaving his chest in one great whoosh, and he lay there, winded, and struggling to breathe.

Mo turned back to Joseph, hatred in his eyes. Joseph took one step back, into a fighting stance, and raised his fists. Mo stood for a moment, hands against his sides, and then turned partly away from Joseph, as if he was going to say something to the assembled gang. But instead he suddenly turned back and closed the distance with a single great leap, his right fist driving for Joseph's face.

Joseph dodged to his left, the blow whistling past his ear, but before he could think of what to do next, Mo counterpunched with a smooth left into Joseph's ribcage. It felt like a cricket ball from a fast bowler, rising and catching him in the short ribs, and he gasped in pain and shock, staggering backwards.

Mo pressed his advantage, grabbing Joseph's shirt collar in his left hand, just under Joseph's chin, and pulling his right hand back in preparation for another blow to the face. Joseph knew he would not be able to dodge it, so he kicked out desperately, the toe of his right boot connecting with Mo's shin. But Mo didn't react, apart from turning up his snarl a notch, and unleashing the blow.

Joseph instinctively ducked his head, to protect his face, and Mo's knuckles connected with his forehead with a loud crunch. The forehead is the thickest part of the skull, but the blow nevertheless left Joseph feeling dazed. He watched groggily as Mo danced away. Mo's face was a rictus of pain, and he was holding his fist in his other hand. The delicate bones in the hand are no match for the thick forehead, and Mo had broken several of his.

But the pain seemed only to enrage Mo more. With a roar of anger, he threw himself back towards Joseph, screaming like a lunatic. Joseph shook off his daze and side-stepped the wild charge neatly, extending a well-timed foot to send Mo crashing to the deck. He stood over the fallen boy, panting slightly. "Had enough?"

But Mo simply turned away from him, face like thunder, and called out to the surrounding group. "Ted! Shorty! Grab him!"

Two boys separated themselves from the group, and walked warily towards Joseph. One of them, presumably Shorty, was very tall, almost as tall as Joseph, but more heavily built. The other was stocky and powerful. Joseph backed away from them, fists raised.

The pair split up, moving to either side of Joseph. Then Ted made a sudden run, his arm sweeping in a roundhouse punch towards Joseph's head. Joseph turned and blocked the blow easily, but almost instantly felt Shorty's arms wrap themselves around him from behind, pinning his own arms to his sides. He struggled mightily, throwing his head back and trying to stamp on Shorty's feet, but the other was too quick, dodging every move. Then Ted walked up, smirking, and unleashed a vicious blow into Joseph's stomach.

The pain exploded upwards, driving his breath out in a huge exhalation and doubling him over as Shorty released his grip. Joseph fell to his knees, eyes watering, gasping for breath. When he looked up again, Mo was standing triumphant, fists on hips. "Have _you_ had enough?" he asked, upper lip curled in savage glee.

Without waiting for Joseph's answer, he turned to Shorty. "Pick him up, and bring him to the railing." Shorty obediently bent over, grasping Joseph under his armpits, and hauled him upright.

Harry came rushing up. "What are you going to do?"

Mo turned to look at him. "Shut up, Harry, unless you want the same!" Harry held his gaze for a moment, then dropped his eyes and turned away. Mo smiled grimly and turned back to Shorty. "I said bring him to the railing!"

Shorty shuffled Joseph across to the railing, and balanced him against it, facing into the void. Joseph hadn't regained his wind yet, and felt weak and dazed. There was an arm against his back, pushing relentlessly. He tried to resist, gripping the railing in his hand, but then other hands grabbed his wrists and jerked them forward, into the void. His feet left the floor, and he was dimly aware of gasps and cries of alarm from the assembled boys, as he was launched into space, falling fast.

The walls and levels of the shaft flashed by as he fell. The rush of air in his face revived him rapidly, and he began to wonder if the airflow from the fan at the bottom of the shaft was increasing. *The fan!* Panic flooded his mind as he imagined himself sliced into a million pieces as he fell into the giant fan.

He tried desperately to move his body in the way he had seen Harry do it, arms and legs spread wide like a star, but slightly bent. He felt a slight reduction in his speed, but the levels still flashed by. Forcing himself to look downwards, into the gloom, he fancied that the movement he saw was speeding up. The throbbing seemed faster too.

After a few seconds, he became convinced that he was slowing down under the upward pressure of the airflow. But he was still falling frighteningly fast. He could see the fan now, deadly flashes flickering on the spinning blades. He had to fight the instinct to bring his hands to his face, to ward them off. *No! It will make you fall faster!*

He edged his arms and legs out slightly farther, willing himself to slow down. It was working, he was falling more slowly— but whether he was slowing enough to prevent an impact with the fan, he couldn't tell. His teeth were clenched tightly together, his jaw locked. He pulled his head back, straining away from the rapidly approaching blades. And still he fell.

Then all hope died. The fan loomed in his vision, it was all he could see, and still he fell. He closed his eyes, ready to scream his last as the cruel blades cut his flesh. *What a stupid way to die.* He felt more ashamed than afraid.

A sudden impact knocked the breath out of him, and he steeled himself for the agony. But nothing else happened. The wind still roared through his hair, but he seemed to be... bouncing?

He opened his eyes. The fan roared mere inches away from his face, the blades a silvery blur. But his vision was slightly obscured by a fine metal mesh. He looked around cautiously. The mesh extended on all sides of him to where it seemed to be attached to the bottom of the lowest level, and he lay upon it, as if on a giant trampoline.

The adrenaline from his near-death experience came rushing into his system, and he began to laugh hysterically. He rolled onto his back and looked up the shaft. Right at the top, he thought he could see faces looking down at him. Then they disappeared.

The fan was slowing, the powerful blast of air reducing. He rolled onto his knees, stood up gingerly, and walked to the edge of the mesh. By jumping up he just managed to grab onto the railing surrounding the lowest level. He pulled himself up over the edge and onto the level itself, looking around him. There was a gloomy corridor leading away from the shaft, directly in front of him.

The adrenalin rush was fading, leaving him feeling dazed and numb. His stomach still hurt from Ted's punch, and the impact with the mesh had scraped his hands and knees. He stared down the corridor, trying to get his fuzzy brain to decide what to do.

I must be on the lowest level of Aeropolis. Need to find a way to get back to the deck. The thought of climbing hundreds of stairs was pretty dispiriting, if he could even find them again. He mentally cursed Mo for putting him in the situation. *What's his problem, anyway? What was he trying to do? He must have known I couldn't be hurt by the fan. So what was the point? Just wanted to scare me, I suppose.*

The sound of increasing airflow made him realise that the fan was starting up again. A crazy idea formed in his head. Without taking any time to consider it, he vaulted over the railing again, ran to the centre of the mesh, and lay down on his stomach, legs and arms spread slightly bent. He tried not to look at the fan blades spinning faster and faster only inches below his face. The blast of air increased steadily, until he felt himself getting lighter on the mesh, and even starting to float slightly. He adjusted his arms and legs, going by instinct more than anything else, and then, suddenly, he lifted off, and went flying back up the airshaft.

His control was a bit haphazard, and a few times he swooped perilously close to the edge of the shaft, but in a surprisingly short time he saw the astonished face of Mo at the edge of the railing he had been thrown from minutes before.

THIRTEEN

IONE

"En garde!" The cry echoed out over the enormous, empty ballroom. Ione stood facing her opponent, her sabre held just in front of her mesh mask. She swept her sword downward in the traditional salute, and then attacked her fencing instructor at a ferocious pace, her sabre whipping through the air. He stepped back steadily, parrying her blows with precise movements of his sword. The clash of blade upon blade rang out over the thump of footfalls as Ione advanced relentlessly. But just as she sensed victory, her instructor delivered a single thrust that pressed the round point of his sword against the padding over her chest. Her heart sank. *So close, yet so far.*

"Very nice, Miss Hughes! Good energy. Although a little wild, especially towards the end. You must always be aware of your opponent's sword."

"Yes, senór," said Ione, removing her mask. She caught her breath as a bead of sweat ran down her cheek. "But I did have you going backwards!"

The instructor removed his own mask. His head cocked slightly as he considered this. "Yes, you are correct," he replied, one eyebrow slightly raised. "But remember that the tactical retreat can create space for the counter-strike, sí? Also, when your opponent is moving forward, you can use that momentum against him, by suddenly standing your ground. He will rush right onto the point of your sword."

Ione nodded. That was exactly what had happened. The sword point had suddenly appeared in front of her, and she had been unable to check her forward movement.

"Muy bueno! That is enough for today. I will see you again next week." With a little bow, the instructor collected her sword, and then turned on his heel and strode rapidly out of the ballroom.

Sighing, Ione turned to go out of the opposite door, to her room. Now that the distraction of the fencing session was over, the unpleasant memory of her abortive lunch date returned. She flinched as she remembered bursting into tears in front of that horrible boy. *He had no right to betray me like that. And after I tried to be sympathetic to him too!* But she knew, deep down, that the real reason for her depression was that Joseph had inadvertently named her greatest fear: that her father was going crazy.

It wasn't just the periodic obsession with people's clothing. He sometimes refused to eat if something about his food seemed wrong to him, and the chef at Top Table had long since learned to make sure that peas served to her father were all exactly the same size, and arranged in a regular fashion. Other obsessions and fixations would arise as well. The latest one related to time: every clock on Aeropolis had to display exactly the same time as that shown on her father's wristwatch. Blake had had to hire someone whose only job was to repeatedly check every clock, one after the other, using a chronometer which Blake surreptitiously synchronised with the wristwatch every morning.

There wasn't anyone that she could talk to about it. Her mother just laughed at her fears. "Of course your father's crazy," she'd say. "That's why we're not together anymore!" When she said things like that, Ione felt a bit foolish, thinking that maybe it was really nothing to worry about. But when other people commented on her father's behaviour, as Joseph had done, then the fear came rushing back.

Even a foam bath did little to lift her mood. Afterwards she lay on her bed, feeling very sorry for herself.

A loud tapping at the door made Ione start. "Who is it?"

"Ione, it's your father."

"Hi Daddy. You can come in," she said miserably, not turning to face the door. Hughes strode into the room. "Do you know where Joseph is?" he demanded.

"I don't know, and I don't want to know either."

Her father raised an eyebrow at that. "What happened? You two have a fight?"

She grimaced. "Something like that."

"Well, when's the last time you saw him?"

"In Top Table."

He frowned. "So you don't know where he went after that?"

She shook her head. "I... left before he did."

Her father rubbed his face, and began pacing up and down, clenching and unclenching his fists. She watched him uneasily. "What's wrong, Daddy?"

"Joseph is missing. We can't find him anywhere. I was hoping he'd said something to you about where he could be."

"No, he didn't." She decided not to explain exactly how Joseph came to end up in the restaurant on his own. "But I'm sure he's safe. Probably just wandered off to look at airships or something."

Her father shook his head. "No, we thought of that already. No sign of him on main deck." He bit his lower lip. "I think he's been kidnapped."

"What? By who?"

"Oh come on, Ione. There's only one organisation out to get me."

"Not the ZA again?"

"What do you mean, again? Do you think the ZA has given up?"

"But why Joseph? What would they hope to gain?"

He shrugged. "I don't know. Maybe they saw you two

together, and thought he was important to me."

"Well, he's not. So there's no need to worry."

He glared at her. "I can't just *abandon* him! Anyway, I knew his father. I have a responsibility." He bit his thumb.

"But what can you possibly do?"

"I don't know. But I'm going to find out what's going on." He turned and stalked out.

Ione's heart sank as she watched him go. The obsession with the shadowy organisation known as the ZA had peaked about a year ago, when her father had been convinced that ZA agents were everywhere, plotting against him, but since then, things had calmed down a bit. Until now.

Of course, the ZA was somehow connected to the Zeppelin company, and everybody knew that relations between the Hughes Aircraft Corporation and the Zeppelin company went somewhat beyond the bounds of friendly competition, but no-one seriously believed that the ZA was engaged in criminal activity. No-one, that is, except her father.

Ione sighed, and turned to stare out of her window. Though she tried to ignore it, the fear nagged at her. It always arose when one of her father's obsessions took a turn for the worse. *Is this it? The beginning of a final descent into madness?*

FOURTEEN

JOSEPH

"I thought Mo was going to bust a gut when you shot up the shaft again!"

Harry was lounging on an improvised chair in the corner of the workshop that the apprentices had converted into a common room. Joseph returned his smile, shifting his perch on an upturned paint tin.

"Yes, I enjoyed that. Although for a while there I didn't think I'd be able to clamber back over the railing."

"Oh, you did a lot better than some I've seen."

"Does everyone get thrown over the railing, then? In this initiation of yours?"

Harry looked slightly embarrassed. "Well, the idea is to time the fan, to fall as little as possible, so most lads jump off the railings themselves."

Joseph raised an eyebrow. "Most?"

Harry gave a short laugh, reddening slightly. "OK, everyone except you." His face fell. "They're not beaten up first either."

Joseph groaned as Harry's words reminded him of his injuries. "What is Mo's problem anyway?"

Harry frowned. "I don't know. He's got a chip on his shoulder, and no mistake. Something about rich people makes him angry."

"I'm not rich!"

Harry looked at him. "Really? Well, you do talk like every rich person I've ever met."

They both looked up as Mo himself walked into the room. His hand was bandaged roughly with an old rag. "Hadn't you better be getting back up to the posh part, then?" he said with a sneer.

Joseph stared him down. "Not really."

Mo turned his attention to Harry. "And what about you? Got no work to be doing then?"

"I've got a break until third shift. Thought I'd show Joseph around."

"Well go on then. Stop taking up space in here."

Joseph looked around the room meaningfully. All the other apprentices had started second shift a few minutes earlier. The three of them constituted the sole occupants of the room.

Harry stood up with a sigh. "Come on, then, Joseph. Let's go."

He didn't want to give up so easily, but Harry was insistent, motioning with his head. Giving Mo a final stare of defiance, Joseph stalked out of the room after Harry, catching him up in the corridor outside.

"Why didn't you back me up? He had no right to kick us out!"

"Come on, it's not worth getting into a fight every five minutes." Harry grinned. "Besides, it's boring sitting in there. There are things I want to show you."

"Like what?"

"You'll see."

Joseph followed his new friend along the corridor and down a stairway. Apart of course from Mo, the apprentices had treated him like a returning hero when he had flown back up the airshaft, and many hands had helped him over the railing as he had struggled to make the transition from flying to standing. It had felt good. As he reflected on this, he became determined not to let Mo blight his mood any more. He jogged ahead to draw abreast of Harry.

"Do you like working on Aeropolis then?"

Harry shrugged. "It's all right, I suppose. Bit boring, all the cleaning and painting. But it's nice to travel 'round the world."

"Do you ever get off?"

"Oh, yeah. Every time we're back in London, I go see me Mum. And I've gotten off in New York twice now. Last time Mr Hughes took us in his airship hisself!"

Joseph frowned at the mention of Hughes. "What's he like, Hughes? I mean, as a boss?"

"There are those that'll tell you he's the Devil incarnate! ZA and the like. But he's always been good to us. Sure and he gets some strange notions, time to time. I s'pose it's because he's so clever, maybe. Me Mum always says genius is close to madness! Not that he's really mad, mind. But he do get some strange notions..."

"What's the ZA? I've heard that name before." Joseph was keen to find out how Monmouth's organisation was perceived on Aeropolis itself, without giving away that he was in effect working for them.

Harry looked at him. "Why, they're a bunch of Kraut troublemakers, if you ask me. Which I suppose you did."

Joseph wasn't particularly surprised by this. "What do you mean by troublemakers?"

Harry stopped, and looked thoughtful. "Don't know, really. It's just what everyone says about them. Something goes wrong on the ship, someone'll say 'Must be the ZA, up to their tricks!' Then we'll all laugh. Well, I say all. There are those who stick up for the ZA. Union types, mostly. They're always saying how the ZA will sort out Hughes. But it's all just talk, far as I can see." He grinned again. "Come on, we're nearly there!"

They turned a corner and came upon a narrow catwalk leading out over the drop of a vertical shaft about fifteen feet across. The catwalk lead to a platform that circled a central column. Harry led the way across to it. As they approached Joseph saw that the column had a narrow slot in it running upwards as far as he could see, and through the slot he could see that the column was hollow. At its base the interior space was filled with a round cage structure.

There was a sort of gate-like door in the wall of the cage, the width of the slot, and Harry turned a handle and opened it. He climbed inside, and then beckoned for Joseph to follow. It was a tight squeeze with the two of them in the little cage, and after Harry managed to get the door closed Joseph felt a little uncomfortable in the tight confines. Harry moved a control lever at his side, and the cage began to rise up the shaft with a shuddering motion. It moved slowly at first, but built speed steadily, until the whir of wheel bearings reached a high pitch and the sound of steel wheels on railings became very loud.

"What is this thing?" Joseph needed to raise his voice over the noise.

"Maintenance hoist."

"Where does it go to?"

"You'll see." Harry grinned excitedly.

The uncomfortable ride continued for some minutes, but at last Joseph felt their upward speed slowing as the noise began to diminish in pitch. This continued until the hoist was moving quite slowly. Eventually it drew to a shuddering halt opposite a catwalk that was a twin of the one they had walked across, hundreds of feet below.

Harry opened the door to the cage, and squeezed out. Joseph followed, feeling greatly relieved to be out of the little cage.

"We'll have to walk from here, I'm afraid." Flashing a quick grin, Harry set off across the catwalk and into the corridor which led away from it. Joseph hurried to catch up.

The corridor led to a stairwell, and the two of them went pounding up the metal stairs. After a couple of flights the stairway came to an end on a narrow landing. Opposite the stairhead a metal ladder was bolted to the wall, leading upwards and through a circular opening in the metal ceiling.

Bright sunlight flooded in through the hole.

Harry crossed to the ladder and started scrambling up it. Joseph followed, emerging into the open air. The ladder was bolted to the outside of a thick column, and although he was climbing through a series of metal hoops that surrounded the ladder, he still felt very exposed. The views of London in the corners of his eyes tugged at his vision but he didn't dare take his attention off the ladder as he climbed steadily upwards.

After a short climb he caught up with Harry on a tiny circular platform, no more than six feet in diameter, that capped the column. It was surrounded by a low railing, and a thin mast rose from the centre, supporting a number of radio antennae high above their heads. Harry was sitting with his back to the mast, looking out. Joseph made his way cautiously over to him on his hands and knees, and then sat down next to him. Only then did he dare look out at the view.

He had expected to be afraid but the sheer majesty of the sight left no room for that. They were on top of the world, all of Aeropolis spread out below them, and beyond the edge of the deck, London and the Thames sparkled in the sunlight. The view from the window in Hughes's offices had been similar, and yet had had a completely different feel. There, it had been like looking at a beautiful image in a frame. Here, Joseph was actually in the picture. He felt the wind on his face, the sun on his skin, even heard the faint noise of the deck operations, and the engines of the airships. It was very peaceful, the cares of the world seemingly left far below.

"This is just amazing."

"Isn't it?" Harry grinned at him. "It's my favourite place. You should see it at night, when we're over a large city. It looks like jewels on a black cloth."

"I'd love to."

"That's the roof of the control room down there," said Harry, pointing nonchalantly at a wide disk about twenty feet below them. So they were higher even than that exalted perch. There was nothing higher, other than the radio masts.

Joseph looked around him, and thought that he'd like to stay forever, and not have to go back down, to face his legion of problems. He shook his head, determined not to let the present moment be spoiled, and turned his face to the sun and the wind, feeling as if he was flying freely through the gentle skies.

FIFTEEN

IONE

After a while she got tired of moping around in her room. She decided there was no point in worrying about her father, or Joseph. There was nothing she could do about either of them, so the best course of action was to continue with her life, and try to distract herself from unpleasant thoughts.

She was walking across the Core, heading for the promenade and a bit of shopping, when she saw him.

"Joseph!" Astonishment coloured her voice.

He turned away from the boy he was walking with, and embarrassment flooded his features as he recognised her.

"Oh, hullo, Ione." His face was quite red, and he looked nervously at the floor.

"What are you doing, Joseph? Don't you know that Daddy has everyone scouring Aeropolis, looking for you? He's convinced you've been kidnapped by the ZA! Where have you been?"

His companion, an apprentice-looking type, stepped forward. "Excuse me, Miss Hughes, but Joseph has been quite safe with us."

She stared at him. "Quite safe? If that's true, how did he

get those grazes on his hands?"

The boy flushed, and looked as if he was about to protest, but Joseph spoke up first.

"It was my fault. I tripped." He exchanged a glance with the other boy.

Ione frowned at them. "I don't believe either of you. I think I should get Mr Thornton. He'll soon find out what really happened."

Joseph looked alarmed. "No, Ione, listen to me, Harry had absolutely nothing to do with my injuries. If anything, he—"

"I helped to treat them," Harry cut in quickly. There was another quick glance between the two of them.

Ione sighed. "Oh, who cares? Keep your stupid secrets then. I don't even know why I was worried about you." She turned on her heel and stalked off.

After going about twenty steps, she had cooled off a bit. She heard Joseph call out to her, but she didn't turn around. She heard running footsteps, and then he was beside her.

"Ione, I wanted to apologise." He looked embarrassed and vulnerable, and she felt her heart melt a little. But she kept up her stern expression.

"What for?"

"For making you worry about me. And also for upsetting you at lunch. I was rude and thoughtless."

Oh, he's sweet. But I'm not going to make it that easy. "So you don't think my father is crazy?"

Joseph flushed. "No. Of course not."

"It was a shame about that. The lunch, I mean. Maybe you can make it up to me."

A wary look appeared on his face. "How would I do that?"

"Well, we must have lunch again sometime."

He frowned. "I'm not sure when I'll be back on Aeropolis, though."

"That's OK. I'll be in London on Saturday. In Kensington Gardens. You can meet me there for a picnic."

"All right." Joseph still looked a bit worried. "What time?"

"How about noon?"

"Very well. Noon in Kensington Gardens. Near the Peter

Pan statue. I look forward to it."

"Me too." She stood smiling at him, secretly enjoying the way he seemed to grow more uncomfortable with every passing second. At last she took pity on him. "How are you getting home?"

He looked comically relieved as he replied. "Oh, I ran into Mr Churchill earlier. He's managed to hire us another airship. Hopefully no-one will try to crash into it on the way home!" He laughed nervously.

She chuckled. "I'm sure that accidents don't happen that often."

"Accidents are one thing. It's the deliberate crashes that worry me!"

"What do you mean?"

"Oh, I'm sorry," he said, blushing again. "Bad joke. I shouldn't joke about such things. Sorry."

She shook her head. "No, I meant, why do you think the crash today wasn't an accident?"

He looked at her, astonished. "Everyone thinks that! Besides, I saw the other pilot. It was deliberate, no doubt about it." Then he suddenly put his hand over his mouth. "Oh, Ione, I'm so sorry! Your father must not have wanted to worry you—"

"It's OK." She forced a smile. "You'd better get going. I'll see you on Saturday."

"See you then." He walked off hesitantly, but she turned firmly on her heel and strode off, thoughts whirling in her head. *If my father believes the crash was a deliberate attempt to harm him, no wonder he's suddenly worried about the ZA again.* And the worst thought of all: *what if he's right, and they* are *trying to kill him?*

SIXTEEN

When she got to the promenade, she found that she was too distracted to look at clothes, and so she returned to the suite she shared with her father on the level below his office. She decided to try to contact her friends in America. *I really need to talk to someone about everything that's been happening lately.*

The radio set gleamed on the desk in her room. She turned it on, watching the valves begin to glow softly as she donned the headset. When the valves were all warmed up she slowly rotated the tuning dial towards the frequency that she and her friends normally used. The cleaner must have knocked the dial when she was dusting. Or maybe her father had been playing with the set in her absence? He was always saying how such an expensive set was wasted on girly chit-chat. She tutted in annoyance, scrolling through the snatched, distorted conversations and bursts of morse code as she traversed the airwaves.

When the band used by Aeropolis Control came up, she was momentarily distracted by the chatter of ships arriving and leaving, seeking and being granted permission to do this and that. A bit of banter between Aeropolis Control and a pilot caught her attention:

* * *

"… Not back to bother us already, are you? Thought you were off to Africa, over?"

"Couldn't stay away from your dulcet tones. Besides, who else would bring His Royal Highness for his monthly turn at the tables, over?"

"Tough job, but I suppose someone has to do it! Mike Victor Niner Fife, maintain current heading and speed, and report when in sight of Pad 6, over."

"Roger that Control."

Ione normally found the gossip of the aircrews amusing, they were like a bunch of old washerwomen. She'd heard someone describe flying as endless stretches of boredom punctuated by moments of sheer terror, so perhaps it wasn't surprising that the pilots took every opportunity to be sociable. But today she didn't feel like being amused.

She scrolled the dial onwards, through bursts of static and snatches of morse code, into a clearer band. Suddenly the silence was broken by a very loud code transmission. Wincing, Ione quickly turned down the volume.

The strength of the transmission meant that it probably originated on Aeropolis, which was odd, since she seldom heard morse transmitted from Aeropolis itself. Perhaps she had stumbled across a navigation beacon ident. She picked up a pencil and began to transcribe the transmission

Dash dot, dash dot dot, dot… the coded beeps, some long, some short, sounded in her headphones, and she translated them automatically into letters, and wrote them down. Her father had gotten one of his own radio operators to teach her morse, insisting that voice alone was not sufficient, and the hours of practice paid off now as her pencil moved fluidly over the pad.

The transmission was the same two phrases, repeated over and over again, with a pause in between for a reply. She had started in the middle of the sequence, but when it repeated, she wrote it down once complete, and on the third repetition, she checked her work, letter by letter.

Storm Tendency, this is Black Rose. Do you read me, over?

She stared at the words, perplexed. *What strange names!* She was about to scroll onwards with the frequency dial, when she heard a reply, much fainter. She transcribed it onto her pad.

Black Rose, this is Storm Tendency. Reading you loud and clear. Make your report, over.

A thrill of excitement ran up Ione's spine as she read the words on her pad. It was clear she was listening in on something that was meant to be private, which must be why they were using funny names. She held her breath, waiting for Black Rose's reply.

Attempt failed. Target unharmed. Await further instructions, over.

As she read the message back, the excitement was overtaken by a hollow feeling of fear in her stomach. Whatever these people were up to, it sounded unpleasant, even dangerous. *What sort of harm do they mean?*

But she didn't have much time to mull it over, as the reply from Storm Tendency came back, fainter, and she had to concentrate to get it down.

Understood. Backup plan already in motion. Stand by for physical message contact. Check usual drop in three days' time. Confirm, over.

Black Rose's confirmation followed almost instantly, loud and clear.

Will check usual drop three days time. Over and out.

There was silence after that. Ione turned off the set with a shaking hand. First the news of her father's ship coming under deliberate attack, and now sinister messages about harming targets were being broadcast directly from Aeropolis. She couldn't but think that the two were somehow connected.

SEVENTEEN

JOSEPH

He spotted Monmouth, or rather his black fedora, as soon as he entered the gardens in the centre of Finsbury Circus. Monmouth was sitting on a park bench, looking out over the bowling green. Joseph marched up to him.

"Why did the ZA try to crash Hughes's airship?"

Monmouth looked up in surprise. "What? That's nonsense! The ZA had nothing to do with that. We would never do such a thing." He frowned. "How did you get to hear about it, anyway?"

"Hear about it? I was on H-1 when it happened! I could have been killed!"

Monmouth gaped at him, his face turning pale. "*You* were on her? But how?"

Joseph flopped down onto the bench next to him. "You told me to spy on Hughes. The opportunity to go with him to Aeropolis arose, so I took it."

"Joseph, I only asked you to report on Hughes's movements, not become his constant companion!" Monmouth paused for a moment, and then continued in a more moderate tone. "Look, I admire your initiative, and I want to hear more about it. But firstly tell me why you think the ZA was involved with this… accident."

Joseph looked at him sharply. "It was no accident! I saw the other ship make straight for us."

"All right, let's say for the sake of argument it was deliberate, although I don't think I've heard anything else to suggest that. Why did you think the ZA was involved?"

"Because Hughes said so."

"He said it openly? In front of you?"

Joseph frowned. "No, I overheard him speaking to Clive Thornton. He asked if there was any sign of ZA involvement. Only he pronounced it differently. Instead of 'zed' he said 'zee'. As Americans do. Because of that, I didn't make the connection at the time. It only struck me afterwards."

"And tell me, did Thornton reply that there was any such sign?"

Joseph frowned, thinking back to the overheard conversation in the Aeropolis control centre. "No, I don't think he did."

"Oh well, there you go. Hughes blames every little problem of his on us. It's well-known on Aeropolis. Surely someone mentioned it to you?"

Joseph remembered his conversation with Harry. "Yes, I suppose they did." Even Ione had said that her father had thought he had been kidnapped by the ZA, when the truth was that he had simply gone off by himself.

"You must know that Hughes is not the most stable individual in the world. Everyone knows he gets these funny ideas from time to time."

"I do know that," said Joseph sullenly. He felt a bit foolish for having accused Monmouth so readily. But then he remembered something else that Harry had said. "But even if Hughes is crazy, the ZA is still known as a bunch of troublemakers on Aeropolis. Why is that?"

Monmouth made a dismissive gesture. "Many people dislike what we do. A lot of it's jealousy if you ask me. Hughes keeps a tight rein on his workers, makes it difficult for unions to function. Part of that is telling people how awful the ZA is."

"Why? Is the ZA a union? You said it was part of the Zeppelin company, didn't you?"

A couple were strolling through the gardens, evidently enjoying the summer sunshine. Monmouth waited until they had passed out of earshot, then turned to Joseph.

"No, I said that I was still helping the Zeppelin company. Which is true. But I work for the ZA, which is a special government agency."

"Which government?"

"The German government. Its full name is the Zollabteilung, which means 'Customs Detachment'. We work to stop people evading their responsibility to pay customs duties."

Joseph shook his head. "I don't understand. How does that help the Zeppelin company?"

"Well, let's go back in time a bit. How much do you know of the Hitler years?"

"We learned about it at school, of course." Joseph scratched his cheek, trying to remember. "Hitler was elected Chancellor for a brief period, then the SA staged a second revolution and had him imprisoned."

Monmouth nodded. "Yes, the SA or Sturmabteilung was led by Ernst Röhm in those days, and he and Hermann Göring realised that Hitler had no intention of carrying out the Nazi party's socialist principles. So they joined forces to bring him down. Unfortunately, by acting against Hitler, they split the Nazi party, and the Social Democrats won the election."

"What does this have to do with the ZA?"

"Well, some of the Nazi leadership decided to promote the socialist cause by working through the new government, rather than opposing it. It's taken a long time, but at last Hermann Göring has created the ZA. Customs duties are an important tool for protecting German workers, and one of the greatest threats to customs duties is Aeropolis. Because of my experience with the Zeppelin company, Göring recruited me to run a special operation against Hughes and Aeropolis."

"So what you're asking me to do has nothing to do with my father!" Joseph felt the anger rising again. "I'm just a pawn in your game with Hughes, aren't I?"

Monmouth looked alarmed, and glanced quickly around him to see who was listening. "Keep your voice down! This has *everything* to do with your father. He was going to leave the Zeppelin company and work for Hughes, but as an agent of the ZA. I believe that Hughes somehow found out, and had him killed."

Joseph felt his anger deflating as the foolish feeling returned. *I've got to stop jumping to conclusions!* "I'm sorry," he mumbled.

But Monmouth didn't seem at all fazed. "That's all right, Joseph. It's a lot to take in, and I think you're doing very well, considering." He sat staring into space for a few moments, then turned to Joseph, smiling. "Enough ancient history. Tell me more about your visit to Aeropolis."

Joseph recounted what had happened at the meeting between Hughes and Churchill. Monmouth listened intently, making notes from time to time in a little notebook. Joseph felt rather gratified that his words were being taken so seriously. He strove to remember every impression and every nuance.

At last he was done, and had told everything that he could remember of his encounters with Hughes.

"So Ione dragged you off to lunch, did she?" Monmouth grinned. "Unfortunate for me that you had to miss the rest of the meeting with Hughes, but perhaps not for you. She is said to be nearly as charming as her mother."

Joseph felt his cheeks grow warmer. "I do like her, yes." He decided not to mention the disastrous end to their lunch. It didn't really matter, because they were friends again. "She wants to see me again, tomorrow."

Monmouth's eyebrows rose. "Back to Aeropolis?"

"No, no, she is coming here. Well, to Kensington Gardens, anyway. I am to meet her there at noon."

"Excellent! You must be as charming as possible. I want her to invite you back to Aeropolis."

"Why?"

"There is something that you need to do for me. When we meet again, say on Monday, and you have secured your invitation, I will tell you what it is." He stood up, looking around carefully. "I'll meet you in the tearoom at King's Cross at nine sharp, I need to take the train to Paris at eleven." He nodded at Joseph and then strode off through the park.

Joseph sat on the bench a while longer, looking at the flowers in the bed in front of him. There was something about his meetings with Monmouth that left him feeling uneasy. He supposed it was just the tension caused by the element of secrecy and the sneaking around, and he reminded himself of how he was helping to track down his father's killer, and that helped a bit. He got up and started walking back to the office, wondering what he should wear to the picnic with Ione the next day.

EIGHTEEN

Saturday dawned bright and calm, with little fluffy clouds in a light blue summer sky. Joseph spent the morning in anxious anticipation. At last it was time to make his way to Kensington by bus, and as he sat on the top deck, looking out at the beautiful day, his heart was pounding in his chest, and he felt slightly dizzy.

It wasn't just because Ione's face had been often in his thoughts since their meeting, he told himself. It wasn't just the memory of her bright eyes and her smiling mouth. He was also nervous about his assignment. Monmouth was expecting him to wangle an invitation back to Aeropolis. What if things went wrong again? What if he completely messed it up, and Ione stormed off again, vowing never to have anything to do with him? The thought made his heart ache.

It won't happen again. Just don't mention her father, and everything will be all right.

The bus was coming up to the Marlborough Gate stop. He rang the bell in good time, but when he got to the bottom of the stairs, he found that the driver had missed the stop, and the bus was continuing along Bayswater Road. The conductor shrugged off his complaints, which made Joseph even angrier. As the bus slowed to take a corner, he decided to jump from the platform. He nearly fell as he landed, but caught himself just in time to raise his fist in triumph at the scowling face of the conductor, before the bus disappeared around the corner.

With adrenalin pumping his heart and a mad grin on his face, he jogged back along the road to the gate. There was a signpost just inside it. Following the sign to the Peter Pan statue, he set off down the path that led past the fountains of the Italian Gardens, with the sluggish expanse of the Long Water to his left. The statue appeared quite suddenly, set back off the path in a grassy glade, facing the water. It was still ten minutes before noon, and Ione was nowhere to be seen.

The boy who wouldn't grow up stood on his bronze tree stump, pipes raised to his lips. Joseph paced around the base of the statue, wondering which direction Ione would be coming from, wanting to see her before she saw him. He checked his watch. Still five minutes to noon. He started to think about what he would do if she didn't come. He dreaded the thought of making his way home in disappointment.

But it never came to that. A few minutes after noon he spied her walking down the path towards him, red hair shining in the sun. She was accompanied by a neat little man in a seersucker suit, who was carrying a large picnic basket.

The appearance of Blake Vanross was a surprise to Joseph. He simply hadn't considered the possibility that Ione would be accompanied. He felt a pang of jealousy, which was absurd on the face of it, as Vanross was employed by Hughes, and therefore almost acting as a servant to Ione. But in his imagination he had pictured only Ione and himself, together in the park. That was obviously not going to happen.

He put aside his disappointment as the pair approached, and smiled. "Hello, Ione. Hello, Mr Vanross. How are you both?"

"Hello, Joseph. Please call me Blake," replied Vanross, smiling in return. But Ione made no reply. She glanced sullenly at Vanross, then looked away, arms folded.

"You'll have to excuse Miss Hughes." Vanross had an amused look on his face. "She's pretty unhappy that her father asked me to come along today. But don't you worry, I won't be in the way. You young folks will still be able to enjoy yourselves."

Ione rounded on him. "But you *are* in the way, Blake! I don't need you. I'm not a child anymore. Nobody follows me around on Aeropolis."

"But this isn't Aeropolis, Ione. This is a large and dangerous city, one that you don't know. You can't simply go wandering around on your own."

Ione narrowed her eyes at this. "Joseph seems to be able to without any problems. And he's not much older than I am."

Vanross sighed. "In the first place, Joseph does know this city; he was born and brought up here." He turned to Joseph. "Am I right?" When Joseph nodded, he continued. "And Joseph is a big old boy. Look at him! Would you want to mess with him? I surely wouldn't."

A dangerous smile started to play on Ione's lips. "Are you saying that I would be quite safe with him?"

Vanross's eyebrows shot up. "Now just you hold on a minute there, young lady—"

But before he could finish, Ione grabbed Joseph's hand, pulling him along with her, and ran off up the path. "Thank you, Blake," she called over her shoulder. "We'll see you later!"

"Ione! You come back here right now!" came the shouted reply. But Ione simply quickened her pace, so that Joseph struggled to keep up.

"Come on!" Ione's face was shining with glee. They ran all the way back to the fountains. Ione led the way to a grassy stretch on the far side of the square building that housed the fountain pump, where she plopped down onto the grass. "He'll take a while to find us here," she said mischievously.

Joseph flopped down next to her. His mind was awhirl

with everything that had happened since Ione's arrival. He felt as if he could hardly keep up with this mercurial girl, but at the same time he felt excited, even exhilarated. He grinned at her, and she laughed delightedly. He felt as though he should say something clever or funny, but nothing came to mind. She didn't seem particularly focused on him, though, as she lay back, resting on her elbows, looking at the trees and the sky and the fountains and the other people strolling in the park. He racked his brain desperately for something to say.

At length he asked the only question he could come up with. "How did you get here?" He groaned inwardly at the lameness of it.

But Ione seemed unfazed. "Oh, we just hired an airship. Poor H-1 will take a long time to fix. There's a landing pad in Hyde Park. We'll be picked up later."

"What time?"

"Oh, much later. Don't worry, we've got loads of time!" She rolled onto her stomach, and looked up at him through her lashes. "What would you like to do, Joseph?"

He wanted to say that he didn't really care what they did, as long as he was with her. But he couldn't, obviously. "Well, we could just relax here like this for a while. We obviously can't eat anything, because Blake has the picnic basket."

She frowned. "Are you hungry? Don't worry about Blake, we'll find him in a little while if he doesn't find us first. I actually meant what would you like to do after lunch? Will you take me rowing on the Serpentine?"

He nodded. "As long as Blake doesn't come as well."

"It's a deal. When I say the word, we both run off again and meet at the boathouse!"

Just then Blake appeared around the corner of the pump house. If he had overheard their plans, he gave no sign.

"Come on, you two. Let's go find some place to have lunch."

They found a nice spot under a tree which overlooked the Long Water, and enjoyed cold roast chicken, sandwiches, and lemonade. After the meal Vanross lit a cigarette and reclined on the blanket as Joseph and Ione horsed around with two sticks which Ione had spotted on the ground. After about the third or fourth painful whack from the end of Ione's stick, it dawned on Joseph that she was wielding it with some skill.

"How do you know how to do that?" he gasped, trying to catch his breath.

"I'm basically practicing my fencing moves on you," she replied, cool and poised with the stick raised and pointing at him.

"Hey, that's not fair!" He was mostly joking, but she frowned at this.

"Ok, I'll teach you some moves then. That'll help to even things up."

She showed him how to stand with his right foot leading and his body turned sideways. "To present a smaller target." She also taught him how to parry her thrusts, but when he tried to strike back, she simply danced back out of his reach, not bothering to parry at all. He tried to copy her light-footed stance, but felt like a leaden elephant in comparison. It was very frustrating.

He suddenly remembered his promise to take her rowing. He indicated the supine Vanross with a jerk of his head. "Shall we head off to our next engagement?" Ione caught on immediately, and with a wicked laugh, raced off in the direction of the Serpentine. Joseph followed, laughing, pretending not to hear Vanross calling after them.

By the time he caught up with them, they were well out in the middle of the lake on a rowing boat, and he could do nothing other than stand at the water's edge, hands on hips. They waved at him gaily, and Ione blew him a kiss. This didn't seem to improve his mood.

Joseph rowed here and there, exploring the Serpentine, and at first Ione seemed content to sit and watch the changing scenery. But after a while she became restless, and turned her attention back to Joseph. "You know what, I think you would be better at fencing if you improved your balance. And boats are a very good way to do just that!" To demonstrate, she sprang to her feet, and balanced sure-footedly as the boat gently swayed and rolled on the water. "Now you try it."

Joseph looked at her dubiously. After shipping the oars, he struggled to his feet. He stood facing her, arms flailing a little from time to time, but managing to maintain his balance if not the entirety of his dignity.

"Very good. Just try to become aware of the weight on each foot, and how it shifts as the boat moves. Don't try to do anything about it, only be aware."

Joseph concentrated on the pressure of the boat's planking against the soles of his feet, noticing how it changed as the boat moved. Without even really thinking about it, the flailing stopped, and he seemed to be moving in unison with the boat, always just enough to maintain his balance.

Ione smiled wickedly. "Very good. Let's make it a bit harder." And she started to shift her own weight, causing the boat's motion to increase in amplitude. She continued to maintain her balance whilst doing this, but Joseph found that his arms were flailing about again, and he felt his balance going. He fell to his knees and grabbed hold of the gunwales to prevent himself from pitching into the lake.

He looked up at her, grinning ruefully. She smiled back, and resumed her seat. Joseph suddenly became aware that they had been staring into one another's eyes for some time. He looked away, feeling himself starting to blush, and busied himself with getting the oars out again to cover his awkwardness. By the time he looked back at Ione, she was staring off at something on the shore. He had a vague sense of disappointment from her, but it was hard for him to know what she had wanted him to do. He rowed back to shore in silence.

All too soon it was time for Ione and Vanross to catch their airship. Joseph suddenly remembered his mission from Monmouth, and it was as if a dark cloud passed overhead and blotted out the sun.

"How much longer will Aeropolis be in London for?"

"Oh, a couple of weeks, at least," replied Vanross. "Will you be returning to us with Mr Churchill anytime soon?"

"I don't know," said Joseph. *Come on, you'll have to do better than that to get an invitation!* "Actually, to tell you the truth, it was a bit of an accident that I came along the last time, so it probably won't happen again." He was gratified to see Ione's face fall at that.

"Gee, that's a shame," said Vanross. He looked at Ione. "Well, I guess you'll just have to come and visit us without Mr Churchill then." He winked.

Ione perked up at once. "Really? Oh Joseph, that would be wonderful!"

"I'd love to return, of course," said Joseph. "But I'm not sure how I would actually get there."

Vanross rubbed his chin thoughtfully. "Well, we get deliveries most days. Maybe you could hitch a ride on one of the cargo ships? Won't be as luxurious as H-1, of course, but it will get you to us."

"That would be perfect." Joseph smiled encouragingly. "When could I come? Would next weekend be all right?"

"I think so. Let me find out who's making deliveries next Friday, and I'll sent the information to you."

"Thank you, sir. So I'll see you next weekend, Ione? So long, and have a safe flight."

After the smiles and waves, walking back along the path towards Marlborough Gate, Joseph knew he should feel satisfaction at having carried out his mission successfully. But he couldn't help feeling guilty and sad, as he remembered Ione's innocent and trusting expression as she smiled and laughed with him. If she discovered that he was spying on her father, she would feel completely betrayed, he knew it. And what if Monmouth was right, and Joseph found the proof of Hughes's involvement in the death of his father? How would *he* feel towards *her* then?

He trudged homewards, his mind a turmoil of unanswered questions and unpleasant feelings.

NINETEEN

IONE

On her return from London she went looking for her father. She found him in his office, behind his enormous desk. Normally he would be busy with reports, or issuing orders to aides. But instead he was taking pencils out of a box, one by one, and lining them up on his desk. Hundreds of pencils already lay on the desk, precisely aligned in serried ranks, and pencil boxes were neatly stacked on the floor next to the desk.

Ione's heart sank. "Hello, Daddy, I'm back from London. Did you miss me?" she asked.

At the sound of her voice, her father seemed to come out of a trance. He turned slowly, blinking at her. At length he spoke. "No. I mean, yes. You bet." He looked at the pencil in his hand, then placed it carefully on the desk. He shook his head, then turned to her, smiling. "Did you have a good time?"

Ione smiled back. "Oh yes, thank you, it was lovely! Joseph will be coming back to Aeropolis next weekend!"

"I'm glad you found a friend. He seems like a good guy."

"Oh, he is. It's so nice to have someone my age around.

All my other friends are back in New York." She frowned. "Which reminds me, have you been able to check out those strange transmissions I picked up a few days ago?"

Her father grimaced. "Oh, that. Well, I spoke to Blake about it, and he doesn't think we ought to worry. Could be a pure coincidence. Or maybe you copied it down wrong."

Ione felt her temper rising. "Of course I didn't! And what does Blake know, anyway? Why don't you ask some of your radio guys?"

He looked embarrassed. "I— I don't want to bother them with this, Ione. It's probably nothing. They'll think I'm letting you push me around. Let's just drop it, OK?" He smiled winningly. But Ione was having none of it.

"It is not nothing, Daddy, it's important! I know it is. You must speak to them about it. Blake's wrong, he must be. You'll see!" She tried to put on her most earnest, imploring expression.

But it didn't seem to work. "Ok, I will, I promise," her father mumbled, but he wouldn't meet her eye, and she knew he was just saying it to get her to stop talking about it.

"Ok, fine, Daddy, whatever," she said angrily, and turned to go. He didn't even try to stop her.

She was so annoyed that she ran straight back to her room and turned on her set again, determined to intercept more transmissions, ones which would prove beyond doubt that she had uncovered a spy ring right there on Aeropolis. She carefully tuned into the frequency which she had written down on her pad, and she waited patiently, but there was no activity, just the endless background susurration of the ether. She stared at the words on her pad, doodling around them.

Storm Tendency, this is Black Rose. Do you read me, over?

She remembered that this transmission, the first, had been the loud one. So that meant that Black Rose was the alias of someone on Aeropolis. But who?

Attempt failed. Target unharmed. Await further instructions, over.

She was still convinced that this was a reference to the deliberate ramming of H-1. Why could her father not see that?

Will check usual drop three days time.

What on earth did that mean? She looked at the words, but no meaning became apparent. Was Will a name? What was supposed to be dropped in three days time? It was like a random collection of words that didn't belong together.

Ione sighed, and returned her attention to the name Black Rose. Suppose it was a code name which bore some resemblance to the person's real name, like a play on words? What would you associate with black roses?

She started to jot down word associations on a fresh sheet of the pad. She wrote *rosebush*, and then *petal*. *Romance* followed, and was immediately crossed out: she had never heard of *black* roses being associated with romance. On the other hand, all flowers had petals. She sighed in frustration.

Suddenly a lightbulb went on above her head, and she wrote down the word *thorns*. Roses were particularly known for their thorny stems. She stared at the word, circling it with her pencil.

Thornton.

It had to be him. She didn't yet know how the *black* part fitted, but it had to, somehow. Turning off the set and removing the headphones, she felt restless energy coursing through her. She opened her wardrobe and cast a critical eye over its contents, thinking and scheming. *Where would Clive Thornton be at this time of day?*

Twenty minutes later, loitering outside Security HQ on Deck 4 and keeping a watchful eye on its entrance, she had her answer. She was dressed in a hastily thrown-together attempt to approximate the garb of the apprentice that Joseph had been with, so as not to arouse suspicion. She was quite proud of what she had achieved, repurposing a pair of brown jodhpurs by knotting an old jumper around her waist, and turning a jacket inside out to expose its dull grey lining. With her hair tied up under an old watch cap of her father's, and a brown woollen muffler wrapped around her neck and partially covering her mouth, she looked like any one of the

STEPHEN WEST

young apprentices found on the lower decks, especially after the judicious application of some dark makeup to dull her porcelain complexion and make her look greasy and in need of a wash.

She caught her breath as Thornton himself emerged from the entrance. Her heart hammered in her chest as he glanced in her direction, but she needn't have worried: his gaze slid right over her, as if he hadn't even noticed her standing there. He paused to light a cigarette, and then strode off down the corridor, acknowledging the salutes of the troopers who were making their way back to HQ. Ione waited until he was a fair bit ahead, and then slouched out of the alcove where she had been waiting, and moved off slowly after him, head down.

From time to time Thornton stopped to have brief conversations with troopers, and when this happened she was forced to find something interesting to look at on the wall next to her. The first couple of times she was lucky: there were noticeboards that she could pretend to study. But then her luck ran out, and there was only a blank wall next to her. She glanced desperately across at the other wall, and saw the doorway to a stairwell. She hurried across the wide corridor and opened the door, pushing past a man in a boiler suit who muttered something under his breath at her, but she didn't care. She walked up the stairs to the next landing, then ran back down again and out into the corridor.

Thornton was nowhere to be seen.

She forced herself to stay calm and fought off the urge to go running madly up the corridor. Walking slowly along the wall, she looked out for alcoves and doorways where he might be. After about twenty yards she came to an intersection with a narrower corridor, and glancing down it, was immensely relieved to see Thornton's cap bouncing along above the throng of people within it.

She tried hard to catch up a bit, but the new corridor was considerably more crowded, and she found it hard to make progress. Constantly dodging, and in some cases colliding with, everyone else, meant that each time she tried to look up

96

to find Thornton again, she was bumped.

Just when she was about to give up in frustration, the crowds thinned out, and she caught a glimpse of Thornton far ahead in the gloom at the end of the corridor. She put on a burst of speed to catch up, but by the time she got to the spot, Thornton had once again disappeared. The corridor was completely empty, and this time, she knew, no amount of desperate searching would find him. She felt the grim certainty in her bones.

She closed her eyes tightly and took a deep breath, resisting the urge to scream with frustration. The moment passed, leaving her feeling close to tears. Sighing deeply, she was about to turn away and retrace her steps home when she noticed a door ajar, a little way down a side corridor.

Probably nothing. Nevertheless she crept closer.

There were low voices emanating from the room beyond the door. She held her breath and slid along the wall to get as close as she dared.

Her heart beat faster as she recognised one of the voices as Thornton's. A triumphant smile twitched the corners of her mouth. She didn't recognise the other man's voice, but it was easier to hear what he was saying, because he spoke with a strident tone in his voice.

"I asked you what you are doing here!" The man sounded aggrieved.

Thornton's reply was difficult to make out, because his tone was low and somewhat placatory. Something about needing to take care? She couldn't be sure.

The other man's reply was even louder than before. "I don't care about that! You had your chance, Clive, and you blew it. It's finished."

Ione nodded to herself. That tallied with the radio transmission: the failed attempt. Although if she was right, that meant that Thornton had been behind the ramming of H-1. She felt a shiver of fear. If he could do that, what would he do to her if he discovered her spying on him?

Suddenly she didn't feel so clever anymore. The whole idea of spying on Thornton, rather than something fun and exciting, now seemed like a very stupid and dangerous thing to do. She started to edge away, back down the corridor, as Thornton's placating, almost pleading tones sounded again.

But before she could get very far, the other man cut Thornton off with an angry exclamation. She heard footsteps, and the next thing she knew, the door was flung open, and a man with dark hair, wearing pilot's coveralls, appeared in the doorway. She shrank down, although it was useless, there was nowhere to hide... and yet, he wasn't even looking out into the corridor. Instead his head was turned back to the room, and he was almost shouting at Thornton, telling him to get out.

Ione didn't need anyone to tell her what a lucky chance she had been given. She turned and raced back up the corridor as quickly as she could while remaining silent, and when she turned into the main corridor, she ran full-tilt, not caring about the noise, and not stopping until she reached the relative safety of the crowded corridors once again.

TWENTY

JOSEPH

At a quarter to nine on Monday morning he walked into the tearoom at King's Cross Station, and ordered tea and a chelsea bun. He took a seat at the window overlooking the platforms, which were wreathed in steam from the locomotives waiting to depart. He had just taken a big bite from the bun when Monmouth suddenly appeared from behind him.

"Good morning," he said, depositing his tray onto the table. Joseph took a gulp of scalding tea to get the mouthful of bun down, then gasped out his greeting, much to Monmouth's evident amusement. "Steady on there, old chap, we wouldn't want you to choke now, would we? Anyway, when you're quite ready, you can tell me all about your little tête-à-tête with Miss Hughes."

Joseph had to admit to himself that Monmouth's condescending style of speech got on his nerves. He frowned while he framed his reply. "It went very well, thank you. I'm to meet her on Aeropolis next weekend."

Monmouth's eyes lit up. "Splendid! Oh well done, old chap. I don't mind admitting that I was prepared to hear of your failure, but this is excellent news indeed!"

Joseph clenched his fists until his nails dug painfully into his palms. *Hear of my failure, indeed!* Why would Monmouth have expected him to fail? He became even more determined to show him. He forced himself to relax. "So what do you want me to do while I'm there?"

"Ah." Monmouth lifted his briefcase onto his lap, and flipped through the papers inside it. He drew out a slim manila envelope. "I want you to make what we call a drop. You need to take this, and leave it in a specific spot, the drop spot, on Aeropolis. No-one must see you do it. I'll tell you exactly where the drop spot is." He held out the envelope for Joseph to take.

"What is it?" said Joseph, making no move to touch it.

"Well now, it's probably better that you don't know that. At least at this stage." Monmouth placed the envelope on the table between them.

"What? Why? How can you expect me to help you, if you won't tell me what's going on?" Joseph felt his patience wearing very thin indeed.

"All right, calm down." Monmouth looked around them quickly, but the tearoom was quiet, and no-one was paying them any attention. He leaned forward, and continued in a conspiratorial tone. "Look, Joseph, this is for your own protection. If you should be discovered, or searched, then you can quite truthfully say that you don't know what is in the envelope, or who it is for. It's standard operating procedure for couriers."

He leaned back. "You're still playing a very valuable role, never doubt that." He spooned sugar into his tea, and stirred it. "But it's best if you know only what you need to." He took a cautious sip.

Joseph picked up the envelope. It was sealed, and had no markings of any sort on its outside. It felt very light, either it was empty or held only a single sheet of folded paper. But what was written on the paper?

"I should warn you that you must deliver the envelope intact and exactly as I have given it to you now. If you tamper with it in any way, I will know about it."

"So this is a test."

Monmouth considered this. "You could say that," he replied after a while. "You will be entrusted with more important duties if you carry out these instructions well." He picked up the envelope. "But this is important in its own right. You will be helping me by doing this, and by that token, helping to bring your father's killer to justice."

Joseph sighed. Monmouth seemed to think he could get him to do anything by trotting out the line about his father every time. "You know, I don't feel that I'm actually any closer to finding out the truth about that. I have only your word that anything is happening at all."

Monmouth stared at Joseph steadily. "It's not just me, Joseph. Lots of people blame Hughes for your father's death."

"Really. Well then, you don't need me, do you?"

Monmouth glared at him. "I don't mean that they think Hughes killed him with his own hands!"

"Then what do you mean? My father died when his airship exploded during testing. It was just an accident!"

"Yes, that's what's generally believed." Monmouth leaned forward, his tone earnest. "But why did it explode? Do airships explode very often?"

Joseph flinched. "No, they don't. But that's because they are usually filled with helium."

"Usually, indeed. But what lift gas was used in your father's ship?"

Joseph felt a heaviness in his chest. "Hydrogen." An image from his dreams flashed in his mind, an image of an exploding, burning airship. He shook his head as if that could clear the picture from his mind.

"Yes, hydrogen." Monmouth's tone was gentle. "Highly flammable hydrogen."

"But there was no choice! Helium was in short supply! The ship had to be tested, so they filled it with hydrogen, just for the test flight."

"Indeed. But why was helium in short supply?"

"I have no idea." Joseph wished Monmouth would drop the subject, he was feeling more miserable by the second.

"Because Howard Hughes was buying up all the helium to fill Aeropolis!"

Joseph stared at the man as the implications flooded through his brain. *He's right. He must be. Aeropolis must use an incredible amount of helium. Hughes used it all up, and my father died as a consequence.* It was a bitter thought.

He rubbed his eyes, suddenly feeling very tired. "So, if everyone knows this, and nothing has happened to Hughes, why do you need me?"

Monmouth frowned in irritation. "You can't be put in prison for buying up helium. I'm merely pointing out Hughes's basic ruthlessness. But I suspect that Hughes went much further than that. I need proof of his direct responsibility for your father's death to put him away. And I need you to help me find it."

Joseph shook his head. "I don't even know what I'm looking for. How do you think he is involved?"

"I don't know for sure. I have a few theories, but I'd rather keep them to myself at this stage, and see how they match up to the evidence you find."

"Why can't you share them with me?"

Monmouth scratched his upper lip. "Because it might influence where you look and what you do. I want to keep myself open to all possibilities. My theories may be completely wrong." He pressed his fingertips together. "This will be a long, slow process, Joseph. I know it must be frustrating at the moment, with you feeling as if no progress is being made. But the truth is that you've made great strides. You are perfectly positioned to see all manner of things on your visits to Aeropolis, and as you bring these things back to me, so the picture will be built up, and I will be able to guide you on where to go next.

"And this envelope, whether you know it or not, is a key step. I want you to take it with you to Aeropolis next weekend, and I want you to find the golden statue of Atlas in one of the arcades that lead off the Core, and I want you to slip the envelope behind the statue's plinth."

Monmouth stood up, put on his fedora, and picked up his briefcase. "Those are the things that I want you to do. I can't make you do them. Only you can decide whether or not you will. I leave it up to you. Should you successfully carry out this assignment, meet me in Trafalgar Square at noon next Monday."

He turned on his heel and strode out of the tearoom without a backward glance. Joseph picked up the envelope and stared at it thoughtfully.

TWENTY-ONE

The week passed slowly for Joseph. He was looking forward to his trip to Aeropolis, and to seeing Ione again, but he felt guilty about lying to his mother. He had told her that Churchill needed him at Chartwell, his country estate, that weekend. And the manila envelope was like a burden on his mind, intruding into his thoughts at inopportune moments. He knew that he probably would make the drop, to prove himself to Monmouth and so get a chance to find out more about what had happened to his father: he was afraid that if he didn't do as he was supposed to, he would never know the truth.

But that didn't mean he liked the thought of doing it. He decided to wait until the last possible moment to make the final decision.

On Wednesday Joseph received a telegram from Blake Vanross, notifying him that he was expected at London Air Park at four pm on Friday, there to meet the captain of the *Lotus Flower*, one Igor Rasmussen, who would give him passage to Aeropolis. Joseph did feel some excitement at that, trying to conjure up in his mind's eye an airship exotic enough to warrant such a name. He imagined that

Rasmussen must be some sort of dashing Russian nobleman, with knee-high leather boots, fearsome mustaches, and, for some reason, an eyepatch. He nurtured these images fondly through Thursday and Friday morning, until at last he could leave work early and make his way to the airfield.

On the train to Feltham, the excitement grew to such a point that it almost, but not quite, drowned out the worry caused by the manila envelope, which was at the bottom of his little suitcase. He got off the train at the station and followed the signs to the air park entrance, enquiring at the gate as to where he might find the *Lotus Flower*, and receiving directions from a man who seemed to find his request highly amusing. Joseph found this odd, but as he made his way in the direction indicated, marvelling at all the airships, large and small, he soon forgot about it.

At last he came up to the landing pad he had been directed to. In the centre stood a modest airship. Joseph could tell from her engine casings that she was not a new model, and she looked to be in poor repair. Rust stained her canvas envelope, running down from corroded docking cables and mooring points, and the paint on her gondola was faded, and flaking in parts, showing dull aluminium struts, or sometimes dry wood. She looked sad, and tired.

Joseph shook his head in annoyance. He must have been misdirected, or had misheard the pad number. This ancient wreck could not be the *Lotus Flower*. He turned around, looking back the way he had come, wondering if he had unknowingly passed the ship on his way here. As he did so his eye was caught by a shambling figure emerging from the old airship.

"You boy! Why you stand there? You go away!" shouted the man. He was tall, with a long, unkempt beard and greasy hair. His long leather flying coat was very old and cracked, and his boots were sadly scuffed and shapeless.

Anger rose in Joseph. "I'm not a boy! And I'll stand wherever I like!"

The man shuffled over to him. As he got closer, it became obvious that, tall as he was, Joseph was taller. Some of the aggression seemed to leak out of him. "What are you doing here?" he grunted, eyes sliding away from Joseph's steady gaze.

Maybe he can help direct me. It's got to be worth a try. "I'm looking for a ship called the *Lotus Flower.*"

To Joseph's astonishment, the man's face lit up with a broad smile, and he turned and indicated his ship with a flourish. "Here she is! Finest ship to sail in air. You are Joseph, yes? My name Igor Rasmussen! I am very pleased to be meeting you, Joseph!" He stuck out a great paw of a hand. Joseph shook it cautiously, trying to overcome the shock of his fond imaginings bursting like soap bubbles in the presence of harsh reality.

He stared again at the airship. Joseph didn't think he had ever seen one less airworthy. It was a wonder Rasmussen was here at all.

"Come, take a closer look!" said Rasmussen. He urged Joseph toward the battered hulk. Hiding his dismay, Joseph walked slowly around the *Lotus Flower*, looking up at the engine nacelles and the envelope. The more he looked, the more faults he spotted. There were missing screws on the nacelles, badly patched tears in the canvas, even a large dent in the gondola wall.

But Rasmussen seemed completely oblivious to his ship's defects, beaming proudly as if showing off a brand new model. "She is good ship, no? Very faithful. We go through a lot together." He frowned at a broken rivet in the gondola sheet-metal. "She need maybe one or two repairs, of course. One day I fix her up." He turned back to face Joseph. "Come on board, we take off soon."

Joseph followed him inside the gondola with a great sense of misgiving. Not only was the interior of the *Lotus Flower* just as faded, worn, and scuffed as the outside, but it was in a terrible mess. Teetering stacks of navigation charts fought for space with dirty dishes and cracked tumblers on the galley table, and piles of dirty clothes reposed on every available bench and couch. Bills of lading and port chits were strewn here and there, or pinned haphazardly to bulkheads, and half-empty boxes of biscuits and sweets spilled their contents over the floorboards.

Rasmussen looked slightly embarrassed. "Sorry about mess, must tidy up... Maybe we go to cabin, is better." He bustled Joseph down the companionway aft, and opened a door. Through the doorway was a small cabin. It was neater, with a bunk and desk below a wide window, though the bare mattress on the bunk was stained and faded, and the window was dirty.

"Please, sit down," he said, indicating the bunk. "We go soon." He shuffled out, leaving Joseph to survey the cabin with distaste. The contrast with his last trip could not have been more acute. *Maybe it's a good thing, and means there won't be any collisions either.* On the other hand, the *Lotus Flower* did appear capable of a catastrophic accident without any need to involve another airship. Joseph sat heavily on the bunk, wondering if he was heading into disaster yet again.

Movement above him caught his eye. He looked up and saw the propeller in front of the starboard engine nacelle start to rotate. Then he heard the whine of the starter motor, and the roar of the engine starting up. This was followed by the sound of another engine, presumably the port one, coming to life. And then finally, the clunks and thunks of the magnetic mooring lines being released. Outside the window, the landing pad began to fall away as the airship nosed into the sky. They were on their way back to Aeropolis.

After a thankfully uneventful flight and a rather hard landing, Joseph found himself unceremoniously dumped by Rasmussen at the passenger terminal. He looked around anxiously. A flash of red hair caught his eye, and he spotted Ione waving at him. Hurrying over to her, he saw she was standing next to a tall woman with the same colour hair, and a face that he had seen a hundred times on movie posters.

"Hello, Joseph." Ione smiled broadly. "I'd like you to meet my mother. Mother, this is Joseph Samson, my friend."

"Hello, Ms Hepburn," said Joseph politely, not sure what to do with the hand that was proffered. He was about to kiss it when Katherine Hepburn seized his own hand and pumped it up and down vigorously. "Hello, young man," she said loudly. "Pleased to meet you." She smiled at him quickly, dazzlingly, then just as suddenly released his hand, and looked around her. "Where is that darned Vanross character?" She spotted someone in the distance, and seemingly without effort, raised her voice to a level not far off that of a foghorn. "Blake! Over here!"

Vanross turned around immediately, and jogged over to join them. Katherine pointed at Joseph's bag. "Ah, Blake. I need you to take this straight up to Howard's guest suite so that we can go directly to dinner." She nodded to him without waiting for a response, and strode off rapidly. "Come along, children," she called over her shoulder.

Joseph felt bad for Vanross but he was not put out in the slightest. He bent down to pick up the bag. "Hello, Joseph. Don't worry, I'll sort this out. You'd better do as she says."

With a grateful nod, Joseph ran off to catch up with the two women. He saw at once that they were headed for the Glass House. At the entrance the maitre d' beamed at Katherine.

"Ms Hepburn! What an unexpected pleasure! I have your usual table, of course." He swept them off to a secluded corner table with outstanding views of the promenade outside the windows, seating Katherine in pride of place, and somehow managing to indicate to Joseph and Ione where to sit without once taking his eyes off Katherine.

After he had melted away with an unctuous bow, Katherine turned to her daughter.

"So things have been pretty interesting around here lately? Your father managed to crash one of his precious airships, people are saying."

Ione nodded. "Yes, although I don't think it was his fault. Joseph was actually on the ship when it happened."

Katherine's eyebrows arched. "Is that so?" She turned to Joseph. "Well, was it Howard's fault then?"

Joseph shook his head. "I'd say definitely not. I saw the other ship approaching, and it looked to me as if they were heading for us deliberately."

"How odd. I do wonder why someone would do that." Katherine's tone suggested she wasn't entirely certain that she believed him.

Ione leaned forward eagerly. "I'm sure that Joseph is right, Mother. I picked up some strange radio transmissions shortly after the crash, I think they might be related."

Katherine laughed. "Really, Ione, you're starting to sound like your father now. I'm sure it was just an accident."

The eager look on Ione's face had disappeared, and she dropped her eyes to her lap, colour showing in her cheeks. But Joseph wanted to know more. "What transmissions? What did they say?"

Ione's hands fidgeted, and she mumbled her response without meeting his gaze. "Oh, they were probably nothing. Just aircrews fooling around, maybe."

He frowned. "Why would you be listening to aircrew radio?"

She went even more red. "Oh Joseph, it doesn't matter! Just drop it, all right?"

"Yes, let's talk about something else," said Katherine. "Have I told you about the movie première I'm taking you to?"

"Oh, Mother, are you serious?" Ione's eyes shone, her upset forgotten in an instant. "Who will be there?"

Joseph sat back, feeling slightly hurt and confused. Ione and her mother went over the guest list of the première for the rest of the meal, and it seemed to him that neither woman was particularly aware that he was present.

After dinner Katherine excused herself to rest up after her journey, and Ione suggested to Joseph that they go for a walk on the promenade that encircled the central structure. He hid his resentment in the hope that Ione would behave differently once away from her mother. They strolled along in the early evening air, looking out at the bustle on the main deck below the railing, which was winding down after the working day.

"I'm sorry I cut you off at the dinner table." They stood side by side, arms resting on the railing. "I just didn't want my mother to hear any more about the radio transmissions. You don't know what she's like," she said with an exasperated tone in her voice.

"That's all right. Trust me, I know that parents don't always understand us."

Ione looked at him then, and they exchanged knowing smiles.

"So what were the transmissions about then?"

"I'm not really certain. They used code names: Black Rose, Storm Tendency. But they talked about harming a target. Or at least, that an attempt to harm a target had failed. And I intercepted the transmissions more or less straight after the ramming of H-1. So they could be connected."

"How did you pick up the transmissions, anyway?"

"I have a radio transceiver in my room. My father got it for me so that I could contact my friends back home in New York."

Joseph was impressed: he had once built a little crystal detector rig but he didn't know anyone who had an actual working two-way radio set. He tried to be nonchalant about it.

"So you just stumbled across two people talking on an open frequency?"

"Well, not talking exactly. It was in Morse code."

Joseph was even more impressed, and slightly intimidated as well. Morse code was notoriously tricky to learn, yet Ione had seemingly picked it up somehow. To cover his discomfort, he decided to go on the offensive.

"But why would you think they were involved in the ramming?"

If Ione was annoyed by this, she gave no sign. "Because of the timing, and the mention of a target being harmed." She looked at him, then moved a bit closer, dropping her voice in a conspiratorial fashion. "Plus, I'm pretty sure I know who the person on Aeropolis is."

"Really? Who?"

"Well, I thought that maybe Black Rose could be a code name for Clive Thornton."

"What! Your father's head of security?" He caught himself when he saw the look on Ione's face, and reduced the volume of his voice. "That's pretty unlikely, isn't it?"

Ione smiled triumphantly. "Well, I thought so too. So I followed him! And I overheard him speaking to someone, a young pilot, about it."

"About the attempt on H-1?"

"Not in so many words, no. But the pilot was very angry with Thornton, saying how he had had his chance, and messed it up."

Joseph frowned. "I suppose that sort of ties up with the radio transmission."

Ione seemed oblivious to his skepticism. "Yes, the only thing in the message I haven't figured out is an instruction to Thornton about something? 'Check usual drop.' I didn't understand that bit." She stared into the middle distance, a perplexed expression on her face.

But Joseph was thunderstruck. Monmouth's last words about leaving the envelope behind the statue plinth, calling it the drop, echoed in his mind. He realised that it must have been Monmouth giving the instructions on the transmission that Ione had intercepted, and the recipient, if Ione was right, was Thornton, who was now expecting to receive the envelope in Joseph's luggage.

It also meant that Monmouth had lied: he *had* been involved in the ramming of H-1. He was using Joseph as an unwitting pawn in a dangerous game against Hughes. *I could be helping him to do something awful, and I wouldn't even have known, if not for Ione.* His hands tightened their grip on the railing as thoughts ran through his mind in a rush.

"Joseph? Are you all right?"

He turned to look at Ione's concerned face. *What do I say? What do I do now?*

TWENTY-TWO

He forced himself to smile. "Yes, I'm fine, thank you. Just a bit tired, I think."

"Of course, you've had full day, going to work, then travelling here on a freighter, of all things. And to top it all off, a dinner with my mother would exhaust anyone!" She smiled ruefully. "I'll show you to your room, and you can get some rest. We'll talk more tomorrow."

As Joseph followed her back into the central structure and up to the level reserved to Hughes, he thought desperately about what he ought to do. One option would be to come clean, confess to Ione and her father. *Tell them I've been spying on them.* But as he said it, his mind shied away from a vivid image of Ione's hurt face, staring at him. *I just can't do that. And how would her father react?* Hughes had been angry enough after the crash with H-1. It didn't bear thinking about.

Ione led them down the carpeted corridor to an imposing set of double doors, opening them with a key. Joseph followed her into Hughes's private apartments, and across the palatial marble entrance hall.

"Here we are, Joseph," said Ione, opening the door onto a magnificent suite. "I hope you'll be comfortable in here. Let me or the housekeeper know if you need anything."

Joseph was so preoccupied with his dilemma that he barely noticed it. "Thank you," he said. "Good night." As he closed the door he was peripherally aware of a look of disappointment on Ione's face, but his thoughts were all-consuming. He went to lie down on the enormous bed.

So if I can't confess, does that mean I just go along with Monmouth's plans? That thought was just as unacceptable. What if Monmouth were planning some terrible atrocity? If he had already tried to crash Hughes's airship, how far would he go? Joseph was afraid to even think it, but there didn't seem to be any way to avoid the conclusion. *Monmouth wants to kill Hughes.*

So what *do I do?* It was impossible to decide when one option was just as unacceptable as the other. The horns of the dilemma pricked him painfully whichever way he turned. But still he turned it over in his mind, going back and forth between the two impossible choices.

After chasing his thoughts around and around for what seemed like hours, he decided to get ready for bed. As he was brushing his teeth in the en-suite bathroom, it occurred to him that he could just do nothing. That way he wouldn't be going along with Monmouth and helping make his plans a reality, but at the same time, he needn't tell Hughes and Ione anything.

He got the envelope out of his suitcase and put it on the bed in front of him. *I could simply tear it to bits right now. Or at least open it first, see what it says.*

And if he read something that required immediate action, what then? What if the message commanded Thornton to stab the magnate as he lay sleeping? He would have to tell Hughes then.

Snatching up the envelope, he was about to open it when he remembered what Monmouth had said. *If I tamper with it in any way, he will know about it.* He paused. He had thought at the time that this meant that the envelope was a test. And thinking about it logically, would Monmouth put something so incriminating into the very first message that he entrusted to Joseph? No, it was far more likely that the message was innocuous, perhaps no more than a code word to let Thornton know it was from Monmouth.

He put the envelope down. *If I destroy it now, I'll just be ensuring that Monmouth won't trust me again. He'll use some other way to do what he wants, and I won't know anything about it.*

Joseph got up and started to pace about the room. Surely it would be far better for him to play along for now, so that in future he would be entrusted with a really important message? Then a sudden thought struck him.

If I make the drop, and then hang around to see Thornton pick it up, I'll have confirmed Ione's theory!

Seized with excitement, he took off his pyjamas and got dressed again. Thornton probably checked the drop at night, when it was less busy, and Joseph himself was going to be spending the following day with Ione, so it would have to be now. He put the envelope into his jacket pocket, and opened the door to his room carefully. It was still an hour or so before midnight but the palatial apartment was in gloom and seemed deserted. He slipped carefully across the marble floor to the front door, and emerged into the corridor outside, patting his pocket to check that he had a key. Seconds later he was in the lift heading down to the Core.

As he had expected, it was virtually deserted. He encountered only a few couples returning from dinner, and a security guard. The statue of Atlas was found easily enough. It stood on its plinth about halfway along one of the arcades that led from the Core to the promenade. The golden figure's bulging muscles showed the strain of holding up the huge globe of the Earth that rested across his shoulders, but Joseph slipped silently beneath it and dropped the envelope down the narrow gap between the back of the plinth and the wall. He then looked around for a hiding place.

Directly opposite the statue was a small portico that stood in front of a shop, some sort of fancy jeweller by the look of it. The portico was supported by two thick pillars, and the left-most one stood very close to the wall of the shop next door, which projected out in line with the end of the portico. Joseph crossed the arcade and discovered that if he sat with his back to the wall next to the pillar, he was in shadow and not visible to the casual observer. Nevertheless he could still see across the arcade to the statue, through the small gap between the pillar and the wall. He settled down to wait.

Despite the discomfort of sitting on cold hard marble, with an equally cold metal wall at his back, he found himself becoming drowsy. He dug his nails into the palms of his hands trying to keep awake, and shook his head vigorously. From time to time the tap-tap of footsteps would echo through the arcade, and he would come onto high alert, but the visitors never stopped, and he was always left alone again.

Then even the periodic footsteps ceased, and only time crept by. He became aware that the marble floor he was lying on was the one in the atrium of the bank, and he realised that he must have fallen asleep waiting for Churchill. There was an insistent tapping sound, which he knew was Mickey, knocking on the great oaken doors of the bank, and he wished he would stop.

"Go away, Mickey," he murmured, and just as he did, the tapping ceased.

With a start, he came fully awake, blinking in confusion. *I'm not in the bank, I'm on Aeropolis!* He glanced out through the gap, and his heart seemed to stop as he saw the figure of a man, bending down next to the plinth of the statue. He held his breath as the man straightened up and slipped something into his jacket pocket. Glancing quickly around him, he turned to face briefly towards Joseph's hiding place, showing his face clearly for a moment, before he hurried away.

Joseph sat back on his heels, feeling stunned and confused. For the light from the lamp over the statue of Atlas had shown the face, not of Clive Thornton, but of Blake Vanross.

TWENTY-THREE

"Is there something wrong, Joseph?"

Ione's concerned face swam into focus across the breakfast table in the apartment's kitchen. He had been a million miles away, but he brought himself back with an effort. "No, not really." He tried to smile. "Just a bit tired. I didn't sleep very well."

She nodded. "Ok, then."

He poured more coffee for himself. "So what are we doing today?"

She smiled. "Oh, there's lots we can do. Just depends on what you like." Her smile turned conspiratorial, and her voice went quiet. "Maybe we can spy on Thornton together."

Oh no! How can I spend the whole day pretending I think Thornton is the traitor? He hadn't managed to work out how to tell Ione about his discovery without incriminating himself. He thought desperately for something else to suggest.

"Actually, I was thinking about a trip down to the lower levels. I wouldn't mind seeing my friend Harry again."

Ione frowned. "Do you mean that apprentice boy I saw you with last time?"

"Yes, that's right, you did meet him. Perhaps we can see if

116

he's free, and do something together."

Ione was looking at him with a strange expression on her face. "You really want to do that?"

Joseph nodded. "Yes. I think it would be fun." He smiled.

Ione did not return his smile. "I see." She stood up from the table, dabbing at her mouth with her napkin. "Maybe you should go by yourself," she said, eyes narrowing. "I've got *such* a lot to do today." She turned and stalked out of the kitchen.

Joseph stared at her retreating back, belatedly realising that he might have been able to handle the situation better. Obviously Ione would not want to go traipsing around the lower levels of Aeropolis with a grimy apprentice. But he hadn't been able to think of anything else to suggest. The strange thing was that he actually quite liked the idea of seeing Harry again, which was possibly why his mind had popped it up as a suggestion. But there was no doubt that, attractive as the option was, it would be better to try to make it up with Ione instead.

He sighed and got up from the table, steeling himself to go and knock on her door and agree to spend the day tailing Thornton. He had just reached the hallway when he saw her march out of the front door of the apartment, coat tails flying, slamming the door behind her.

He rolled his eyes. *So much for that idea.* He trudged off to his bedroom, and got washed and dressed. He had a vague idea of trying to find Ione, but the more he thought about it, the more he realised that he was going to have to decide what to do about Monmouth and his spy.

At first the knowledge that the agent was Vanross and not Thornton hadn't seemed to change anything, but the fact that Vanross was Hughes's right-hand man now made Joseph wonder how much more information Monmouth could possibly require on Hughes. If Vanross didn't know something, how on earth could Joseph be expected to stumble across it?

So Monmouth must want Joseph for something else. The question was what.

The answer was certainly not obvious to him. After much thought, he decided that he probably needed more information, and that the best way to get it was still to act as if he knew nothing about Vanross and to pretend to go along with Monmouth's plans. Perhaps the next time he would be entrusted with a delivery of real significance, some form of incontrovertible evidence, and he could take it to Hughes, saying he had spotted it lying behind the statue, and in that way unmask Vanross without incriminating himself.

He felt much happier after reaching that decision. The only question that remained was what to do for the day, now that he had managed to once again mess things up with Ione, and he was effectively alone on Aeropolis once more. His original plan to visit Harry still seemed attractive, and he was fairly sure that he could make his way back to the lower levels without getting lost.

Ten minutes later he was in the Core and heading down one of the access passages. This time, he felt quite the expert as he consulted the location markers painted on the corridor walls, but he still made a few wrong turnings and ended up in some unexpected places before he finally found his way to the apprentice common room. Unfortunately, it was deserted, apart from a morose-looking Mo, who rolled his eyes as Joseph walked in.

"Cor blimey, if it ain't the toff again. What are you doin' here?"

Joseph's heart sank, but he was determined not to let Mo intimidate him. "I'm looking for Harry, actually. Have you seen him?"

Mo grinned unpleasantly. "He ain't here."

"I can see that. I was wondering if you knew where he was."

"Why the hell should I help you?"

Joseph began to get annoyed. "Maybe to say sorry for the way you treated me the last time we met!"

Mo looked defensive. "Ah, come on. We've all been through the initiation. Ain't my fault if you can't handle it."

Joseph put his hands on his hips, leaning forward. "In the first place, I *did* handle it, if you remember. And secondly, the initiation *you* went through didn't involve being thrown off the balcony after being beaten up, did it?"

Mo looked away, refusing to meet his eye. But Joseph was insistent.

"You treated me differently, didn't you?"

Mo jumped up, and made as if to walk past him. Joseph moved to block his path. In place of the usual rage he was feeling a quiet but implacable determination. Mo looked up into his eyes, face starting to twist into a snarl, but it sort of melted away in the face of Joseph's glare, and he dropped his gaze and turned away, shoulders slumping.

"Yes! All right, I shouldn't have done that." Mo glanced at him, biting his thumbnail. "I don't know why I did it to you. Sometimes I just get so angry, you know?"

Joseph nodded, surprised by a sudden feeling of understanding. "Yes," he said softly. "I think I do know. When I lost my father, I was very angry a lot of the time. To tell you the truth, I still get angry more often than I like to."

Mo nodded. "I ain't never really known me dad. Me mum says he left when I was small. Sometimes I think I remember him, but then I'm not sure." He shrugged. "Dunno why I should care though. But I do."

He stood up straight, and walked over to Joseph, a slight swagger in his stride. Joseph swallowed, and took a step back. But Mo put out his hand, his expression intent. "I apologise for what I done, Samson. You're a good egg."

Joseph took his hand and shook it, trying to match Mo's firm grip. "That's all right."

Mo nodded, releasing his hand. "Anyway, you're out of luck as far as Harry's concerned. He's on a double shift, doesn't knock off till midnight."

Joseph nodded, disappointed. He turned to go, wondering what he would do for the rest of the day. Maybe he could try to get a ride home earlier than planned.

"Hey, Samson. Ever been flying in a aeroplane before?"

TWENTY-FOUR

On the way up to the deck, Mo explained that he sometimes helped the mechanics who looked after the squadron of Spitfire fighter planes that Aeropolis used for air defence.

"I'm good mates with one of the pilots. Andy Rowan. His dad owns the engineering firm where my uncle is the foreman. He sometimes takes me up in the Spitfire trainer, if he's not busy."

"So you'll let me go in your place?"

Mo nodded. "Looks like you haven't got anything else to do, with Harry working."

"Thanks, Mo. I really appreciate this." Joseph was actually feeling a bit apprehensive about the flight, but he wanted to encourage Mo's latest behaviour.

"Ah, it's nothing really. To be honest, I'm a bit bored of flying now." Mo gave a short laugh. "Anyway, when we get to the hangars, just let me find Andy first and have a chat with him, all right?"

Joseph nodded his agreement, and waited on one side of the enormous main hangar opening. After a few minutes, a pilot in a flyer's jumpsuit came striding up, beaming at him.

"Hello, young man. I'm Andy Rowan. Are you ready to

do some flying?"

Joseph put out his hand in greeting. "Joseph Samson, sir. Pleased to meet you!"

"Please call me Andy," replied the young ace, with a grin. "Let's get going, shall we?"

Joseph nodded happily, trotting to keep up as Andy walked rapidly across the deck towards a Spitfire that had an extra canopy behind the usual one. A double ladder gave access to the open cockpits.

"Climb in the front seat," said Andy, as he made his way up the rear ladder. When Joseph got the top of his ladder, Andy was waiting to help him in.

"There's no floor, Andy!" The interior of the cockpit was an incomprehensible collection of functional controls, pipes, switches, and indicators, and below the seat was nothing but the exposed structure of the airframe.

"Just step down onto the seat, then put your feet onto the rudder pedals as you sit down. You don't need a floor!"

Joseph did as he was told, placing his feet in the silver stirrup-like structures that he presumed must be the pedals. Soon he was strapped into the front seat. It was a tight fit, and his head, clad in a leather flying helmet, only just barely cleared the canopy when it slid closed.

"You should have a good view from there," said Andy, squeezing in behind him. "Just don't touch any of the controls! Move your feet lightly when you feel the pedals move." He slid his own canopy closed. With a whine from the starter motor the Rolls-Royce Merlin engine clattered into life, and they were taxiing towards the runway threshold.

After lining up on the runway centre line, Andy braked the aircraft to a smooth halt. Then the loping idle of the big V-12 rose to a roar, the whine of the supercharger clearly audible in the cabin, as the airflow from the propeller whooshed over the canopy. The little aircraft was vibrating, shaking, virtually straining at the leash. Then Andy released the brakes, and Joseph was pressed back into his seat by the sudden acceleration. The fighter raced off down the runway, nose pointing at the sky until the tailplane reached flying speed and lifted the tail off the deck.

Then Joseph could see the end of the runway, approaching at alarming speed. But Andy held the plane firmly on the deck. Faster and faster they went, racing headlong to the edge, and beyond it was nothing but blue sky. Joseph's heart hammered in his chest. Seemingly at the last possible second, Joseph saw the stick move back sharply between his knees, and the plane rotated nose up and zoomed off the deck like a homesick angel.

Joseph whooped with delight. The exhilaration of the effortless soar into the blue sky was like nothing he had ever experienced.

Andy's voice crackled over the headphones. "Quite something, isn't it? I never get tired of that!"

He banked the aircraft into a steep left turn, and Aeropolis came into view, shockingly far behind and below them already. The plane dropped into a shallow dive and ate up the distance effortlessly, and then they were skimming past the control tower, so close Joseph could see the controllers through the windows. One of them began telling Andy off, his voice tinny and strident in the headphones. Andy laughed, waggled his wings, and then Aeropolis was far behind them again, as they soared into the blue.

After climbing for a few minutes, Andy levelled off. The green patchwork quilt of the home counties lay far below, hazy in the afternoon sun.

"Joseph, how would you like to do a bit of flying?"

Joseph's heart raced. "I'd love to, Andy! But is it safe?"

"Perfectly," came the reply. "Just grab the stick, lightly. Don't touch anything else for now."

Hands shaking, Joseph reached out and grasped the round ring that surmounted the control stick in front of him. He could feel the soft vibrations from the air rushing over the control surfaces, trying to move the stick slightly this way and that.

"OK, I'm hands off," said Andy. "You're in control."

Joseph gently nudged the stick left. Instantly the plane dropped its left wing, moving into a smooth turn. Something felt slightly off. For some reason he couldn't explain, Joseph's left foot nudged the left rudder pedal. The turn tightened slightly, and Joseph no longer felt as if he were leaning over.

He smoothly returned the stick to the centre position, bringing the pedals even as the plane straightened out, perfectly level.

"Joseph, have you ever flown a plane before?" asked Andy.

Joseph shook his head. "No, never. First time ever in a plane."

There was silence. Then Andy spoke again. "Who told you to coordinate the turn with the rudder?"

"No-one. It just seemed like the right thing to do."

"Well, it most certainly is. But most people take some time to work out how to do it, even after they've been told to. Roll right, a bit harder this time."

Joseph nudged the stick to the right, a bit more firmly. He felt the ailerons bite into the airflow, pushing back, but he held the stick until the horizon stood at a forty-five degree angle in front of him, and then he allowed the pressure to guide the stick back to the centre a bit. Again he used the rudder pedals to get the turn to feel right. He overshot a bit on his first attempt, but then corrected.

"Very nice. Now level out."

Joseph smoothly returned the plane to straight and level.

"You have a very good feel for flying, Joseph. I don't think I've ever seen anyone pick it up as quickly as you have."

Suddenly the plane's smooth equilibrium was interrupted by violent buffeting. The right wing shot upwards, and Joseph fought to keep it level, his heart pounding.

"Easy, there. I've got her." A strong and insistent force through the stick told Joseph that Andy was back in control. He released the stick with relief.

"What's happening?"

"Just some turbulence. The afternoons can get bumpy in summer, as the heat from the land rises up. I'll take her down a bit."

Andy threw the little fighter into a turning dive, making Joseph's stomach feel very odd. But soon they were in smoother air.

"I'm going to head back now," said Andy, lining up the plane on a heading a bit to the left of the distant speck that was Aeropolis. After a few minutes, however, when Aeropolis had grown large enough to show a distinct shape to Joseph, he altered course slightly to aim dead-on.

Soon they joined Aeropolis's traffic patterns, with lots of instructions from Control in the headphones. Andy turned onto final approach, the runway lined up ahead of them, and the engine noise reduced. Then the little plane decelerated sharply, pushing Joseph forward against his shoulder straps, and they started to drop more steeply towards the runway threshold.

Joseph stared at the approaching main deck of Aeropolis. There was the familiar hive of activity swarming around the multiplicity of airships. It was all growing larger at alarming speed. He felt himself flinch away from the impact.

The main wheels hit the runway right on the white-painted lines of the threshold. Andy braked savagely, throwing Joseph forward against his straps again, but it seemed impossible that they could stop before the plane ploughed into the hut at the end of the runway.

But Andy braked even harder, making the straps cut painfully into Joseph's shoulders. By the time the little plane reached the end of the runway it was doing no more than a fast taxi. Andy turned off in a wide circle to line up with the other fighters and cut the engine, which died with a final shudder that shook the plane.

"That was amazing!" Joseph's voice sounded very loud to himself in the sudden silence. The excitement had made his heart race, and he tried to calm down.

"Yes, it's quite something. No matter how many times I do it, it's always special. Joseph, you're a natural flier. Have you ever considered becoming a pilot?"

Joseph winced. *How to explain?* "My father was a pilot," he said guardedly.

"Was? What does he do now?"

"He's dead. He was killed in an airship explosion."

"Ah. I'm very sorry to hear that."

"Thank you." Joseph sighed. "Anyway, because of that, my mother is very against my having anything to do with aircraft—"

"Your mother?" Andy cut in. "Look, Joseph, if you don't mind some friendly advice, it's one thing to say you're not keen on flying because of what happened to your father. But you're a man now, you need to make your own decisions. It's your own life, not your mother's."

Joseph sat in the Spitfire cockpit, and remembered the way his heart had soared as the plane raced up into the sky. As though he belonged up there, and was going home. He had never felt anything quite like it before. He wanted to feel it again.

He was in a thoughtful mood when he let himself into the apartments. He wanted to go to his room and think long and hard about what Andy had said, but before he reached it, Ione appeared at the door of the sitting room.

"Hello, Joseph." She looked somewhat subdued.

"Hello," replied Joseph. "Did you have a nice morning?"

She looked at him with a pained expression on her face. "Not really." She sighed. "Why don't you come in here?"

Joseph followed her into the sitting room, which was enormous. He sat down on one end of a sofa that stretched almost the entire length of one wall. It was very square and black. Ione sat opposite him in a white leather chair with a curved chrome frame.

"I'm sorry I walked out on you this morning." Ione bit her thumb. "It wasn't a very hospitable thing to do."

Joseph nodded. "It's all right. I wasn't being a very good guest, I suppose."

She looked at him with amusement in her eyes. "Maybe we should just forget about this morning, and start again."

Relief rushed through him as he nodded happily. "Yes, let's do that." He smiled.

She smiled back, then jumped to her feet. "Come on then, let's go get some lunch." She was her old energetic self again, moving at top speed, and Joseph had to hurry after her, feeling very glad that they were back on friendly terms.

They had lunch in a little café just off the promenade, and by some unspoken agreement Ione didn't mention Thornton, and Joseph said nothing about Harry. He did tell her about his adventure in the Spitfire, though, and she listened in rapt attention.

"Maybe you should leave the bank, and become a pilot," she said at the end. "It sounds like you have a natural talent for it."

He nodded. "Yes, that's what Andy said I should do, funnily enough." He paused. *If I tell her I'm worried that my mother won't let me, she will think I'm a bit of a baby.* "I'm not sure if it's right for me, though. I do have good prospects at the bank."

Ione nodded. "Oh, flying's not for everyone, that's for sure." But Joseph thought he caught a hint of disappointment in her voice. *And maybe that's right. I should be able to decide for myself.*

After lunch Ione had to get ready to accompany her mother to the première, so Joseph spent the afternoon wandering around the promenade, looking at all the aircraft, and pondering his future. He had been offered a lift back to London with Ione and Katherine, so he made his way back to the apartment to pack. As he walked through the front door, he found Ione in the entrance hall, and the sight took his breath away.

She was wearing a long, flowing dress made of some incredibly light, filmy material, and her hair was up and sparkling with jewels, the flaming red setting off the rich green colour of the gown in a way that drew his eyes irresistibly. She was a vision, like nothing he had seen before.

She turned to face him. "Hello, Joseph. Do I look all right?"

His mouth was dry, so he nodded at first, and then managed to get some words out. "Yes. You look… very nice.

126

Lovely." He felt himself blushing, but Ione just smiled.

On the flight back to London, Joseph was caught up in the excitement of the première. But Ione and Katherine went off in a limousine, and he was left to make his way home from the airfield on the night bus. When he at last turned into his road again, the black feeling hit him like a physical blow. It was as if he were waking up from a beautiful dream, to find himself back in depressing reality.

TWENTY-FIVE

"Good morning, Joseph. How was your trip to Aeropolis?"

Joseph froze as he held out the post to Churchill, his hand half-extended. But the Chairman simply chuckled. "Oh, don't look so alarmed, dear boy. I shan't tell your mother. Your secret, as they say, is safe with me." He winked broadly.

Joseph recovered his composure, and deposited the post on Churchill's desk. "But how did you know?"

"Oh, I have my spies. Anyway, how was it?"

"I enjoyed it very much, sir. I got to fly in a Spitfire!"

"Indeed? I had rather hoped to hear more about Miss Hughes and her famous mother, but never mind, this is most interesting. A Spitfire, you say? How exciting."

"Yes, it was. The pilot let me have a go at the controls. He said I was a natural flier."

Churchill's eyebrows shot up at that. "Well, well. But then I suppose that you have it in the blood. People always said your father could fly a barn door if you attached an engine to it."

Joseph smiled at this, but the smile soon turned to a frown. "I think I do take after him. But I don't think that my mother wants me to."

Concern creased Churchill's forehead. He took out a cigar, nipped off the tip and end, and spent a few moments lighting it. At length he sat back, blowing out clouds of fragrant blue smoke. "I cannot deny that you are correct in your surmise. After your father's untimely death, your mother came to me about finding work for you. I said to her then that there must be many in the aviation industry who would gladly help out the son of Morgan Samson. But she would not hear of it."

"I didn't know that. About her coming to see you, I mean."

"I've known your mother since before she met your father. She worked for me as a typist when I was in Parliament. In fact she was much more than just a typist, she helped me immensely with my speeches. So when she asked me for help, I was only too glad to give it."

He took another puff. "The thing is, Joseph, I don't think that you are very happy here. Are you?"

Joseph rubbed his forehead. "I don't wish to sound ungrateful, sir."

"Well, I don't think it's a question of that. You've applied yourself and worked as hard as anyone could expect, and from that alone no-one could accuse you of ingratitude for the opportunity. But you cannot help the way you feel. And I noticed, on that first trip to Aeropolis, that you came alive in a way I've never seen before."

Joseph rubbed his chin. "Yes, that's probably true. But I know that my mother is so afraid that she'll lose me as well. It's as if I have to continue on this safe path she's mapped out for me, to keep her from worrying."

Churchill looked thoughtful. "It's an admirable thing, of course, to honour your parents. It's one of the Ten Commandments, after all. But you do need to be true to yourself as well. Not so?"

"But how can I betray my mother like that?"

"Is it really betrayal, to follow your dreams?"

"It will certainly hurt her, cause her worry and concern."

"What somebody may feel in response to our actions is certainly something we need to consider. But we can never let it determine our actions automatically. What if your mother decided it wasn't safe for you to leave the house? Would you honour her wishes then?"

"No, of course not. But that would be irrational."

"Some might say that not allowing your son to choose his own path was irrational too. And it may be that in time your mother would come to see this herself. Sometimes grief has a too-strong hold over us. You might be giving her the tool to break its grip."

"But she's lost so much! It's just not fair."

"Fair? No, it's not fair. But, do you know, I've often thought that the unfairest thing of all, is the idea that things should be fair. Because, in this world we live in, the only certain thing seems to be unfairness. You can rely on very little, other than that you are sure to find people who don't have the things others do, because they lose what little they did have, or never got anything in the first place. There are helpless babies born blind, crippled, deformed. Innocent children suffer and even die.

"No, life is not fair. So I decided long ago to do two things, as often as I remember to do them. The first is to try to help those who have not. And the second thing is to be thankful for the things that I have.

"Be thankful for the gifts that your father has left you, and use them."

Joseph looked at Churchill. "So you think I should rebel against my mother?"

Churchill smiled. "Yes. By all means, be rebellious! The job of the young is to rebel. When I went to Cuba as a young man, my mother was terrified I would be killed in the fighting, but I wanted to see action. And by God I did. I've been under fire countless times, in India, and in the Sudan, and in South Africa I was captured by the Boers and even managed to escape from their POW camp. If I'd let my mother tell me what to do, well, I wouldn't be the man I am today.

"Think about what I have said. Opportunities in life are seldom repeated. You have been dealt a terrible blow. Don't turn away from the opportunity to have some of the sting of that blow removed."

Joseph nodded, feeling a little overwhelmed by all that he had heard. "I will think about it very carefully, sir. And thank you for your interest."

"That's all right, young man. I wish you the very best in whatever you decide to do. Now, if you'll excuse me, I have a tedious board meeting to attend!"

Joseph walked out of Churchill's office feeling both excited and apprehensive. Maybe it *was* possible for him to have the life he wanted. He just had to face down his mother, and overcome his feelings of guilt.

All of these thoughts evaporated when he walked into the post room and saw Mickey standing in front of his pigeon hole, putting something into it. He rushed over.

"What do you think you are doing?"

Mickey turned smoothly, his body blocking access to the pigeon hole. "Oh, hello, Samson," he said, with his usual smirking smile. "Been neglecting your duties again?"

Joseph ignored this. "What were you doing in my pigeon hole? What have you put in it?"

"Ah, now Samson," he said, with an exaggerated, almost didactic tone, "the question ain't what have *I* put in it. The question is, what have *you* put in it?"

Joseph scowled. "Nothing that oughtn't to be in there, and you know it."

Mickey scratched his chin thoughtfully. "Well, the thing is, I thought I spotted something awry just now, and I was just having a little butchers' at it, when in you walk. Not to worry though, it can wait until Miss Honeywell gets here."

Joseph felt a cold chill pass over him at the mention of the office manager. "What do you mean?"

"Oh, I sent Neddy to go call her as soon as I spotted the... *questionable item.* In your pigeon hole." Mickey affected a careless air as he spoke, but his eyes were watching Joseph closely.

"What is going on in here?" The strident tones of Janice

Honeywell filled the post room as she marched in, followed by Ned, who had a snide grin on his face.

"I was just tryin' to prevent Samson here from tamperin' with the evidence, Miss Honeywell," said Mickey, his face a picture of earnestness. But Miss Honeywell narrowed her eyes at him.

"Is that so? Well, there's a first time for everything, I suppose." She turned to Joseph. "What were you trying to do, Joseph?"

"When I walked into the post room I saw Mickey fiddling about in my pigeon hole, miss, so I just asked him what he was doing. I haven't tried to take anything out."

"With the way he is standing, you'd have no chance to anyway. What were you doing in Joseph's pigeon hole, Mickey?"

"I saw something suspicious, so I decided to investigate, miss."

"What do you mean? Show me." She stepped forward, adjusting her glasses.

Mickey stepped aside, and indicated a sealed white envelope.

"What's suspicious about that?"

"There's no address on it, miss. So it can't be something that Samson is supposed to deliver or nothing."

Miss Honeywell picked up the envelope, and turned to Joseph. "What is in this, Samson?"

Joseph shook his head. "No idea. I've never seen it before, miss."

She frowned, turning it over in her hands. There were no markings on it anywhere. It was made of a heavy cream textured paper. The flap was sealed. She picked up a paper knife and slid it under the flap, expertly cutting it open, and then removed from the envelope a single banker's draft. It was drawn on the City & Empire Merchant Bank, of course, and it was blank and unsigned, except for the payee line, which bore two words in block capitals.

JOSEPH SAMSON

Joseph felt faint, and he had to lean against the cabinet

holding the pigeon holes. But Mickey leaned forward, a triumphant look on his face.

"Cor, miss, look at that! He ain't decided how much money he's going to try and steal yet, but he's gone and filled in his name all right!" A sneer twisted his grin as he looked across at Joseph. "Shall I run and fetch a bobby then, miss?"

"I don't think we need to involve the police quite yet," snapped Miss Honeywell. She put the draft back into its envelope and then tucked it under her arm. "Mr Samson, you will come to my office tomorrow morning at eight sharp." And with that she turned and left the room.

Mickey stared after her with an expression of bafflement. Then he turned back to Joseph, trying to recover his familiar sneer.

"Well, Samson, looks like you're for the high jump and no mistake. If I were you I'd scarper now. She's bound to have the police waiting in her office tomorrow."

A quiet voice in Joseph's head urged him to stand his ground, and not give Mickey the satisfaction of seeing him leave. But another part of him, the greater part, had simply had enough, and he found himself stumbling from the room and down the stairs. *I need to get some air.* He stepped out onto the street, into the noon sunshine. A bus was passing, heading for the National Gallery, according to its route indicator. Joseph followed its progress down the street, as an uncomfortable feeling of having forgotten something stirred inside him.

The National Gallery. What is it about the National Gallery that I'm forgetting?

It burst upon him with a feeling of panic. *The National Gallery is above Trafalgar Square! The meeting with Monmouth!*

TWENTY-SIX

He stared at his wristwatch. It was a quarter before noon. He ran full-tilt down the street towards the bus stop, where another bus was just pulling up. It was close, but he jumped onto the rear platform just as the bus pulled away. Panting slightly, he made his way to the upper deck, and found an empty seat.

The journey was spent rehearsing what he would say to Monmouth. *I made the drop as you asked. I did it the first evening. I found the statue easily. I'm sure that no-one saw me.* He went over it again and again, trying to anticipate any questions that Monmouth might have, any inconsistencies that might trip him up. *I must remember not to let anything slip about Vanross.* In a way he was glad to have something else to focus on, it helped take his mind off the business with the banker's draft.

All too soon, his stop was next. He ran nervously down the stairs and nearly tripped at the bottom, stumbling across the rear platform and catching himself on the pole just as the bus shuddered to a halt.

As the bus pulled away in a cloud of diesel fumes he crossed the road and surveyed Trafalgar Square spread out below the National Gallery. He spotted Monmouth leaning against the plinth of one of the famous lion statues, and descended the stairs to cross the square. The shadow of Nelson on his column fell across him, and he felt a sudden chill despite the warm sunshine.

"Hello, Joseph." Monmouth was wearing a pair of dark glasses which hid his eyes. He stubbed out his cigarette against the statue plinth, and stepped forward to meet Joseph. "Well done. You completed your mission."

Joseph nodded. "Yes, it seemed to go well."

Monmouth cocked his head, reaching out to squeeze Joseph's upper arm. "Are you all right? You look a little glum. Everything OK at work?"

"Oh yes, everything is fine," he said. He certainly didn't want Monmouth to know about his work problems.

"What is it then?"

"All right, I'll tell you. I just don't feel comfortable spying on Hughes. I feel as if I'm betraying Ione's trust."

Monmouth nodded at this, and relaxed his grip on Joseph's arm. "Well, I suppose I can understand that. You have developed feelings for the girl, yes? Can't say I blame you." He scratched his chin. "Of course you don't need to carry on if you don't want to. I'm sure I can find other ways of finding out what happened to your father."

"No, I do want to continue, of course. I will do anything to bring my father's killers to justice. It's just difficult sometimes. But I can handle it."

Monmouth smiled. "Of course you can! You've done very well. I think you're ready for the next task."

"What is it?"

"It's another courier job, I'm afraid." He bent down and opened the briefcase at his feet, removing something from it, and straightened up again. Joseph was handed a small but quite heavy package, wrapped up in brown paper and sealed with string and sealing wax. He had been expecting a letter, and was a little taken aback.

"Now, again, whatever happens, this package must not be tampered with. Deliver it to the drop point on Aeropolis, but do not open it."

Joseph nodded. He presumed there was no point in asking Monmouth what the package contained, as he would simply be given the same guff about not being told for his own protection. "How will I get back to Aeropolis?"

Monmouth grinned. "Well, I was rather hoping that the charming Miss Hughes would invite you back again. But if that's not the case, I've taken the liberty of arranging you transport on a freighter which is leaving London Air Park next Friday evening. She's the *Lucky Lou* and her skipper is expecting you. Name of Nelson Shaw."

Joseph nodded, and took the package under his arm. "All right. Shall we meet again next week?"

"We shall indeed! Let's make it at Seven Dials, near Covent Garden. Monday at noon?"

"See you then."

"Good luck, Joseph."

The unexpected size of the package posed a problem that Joseph spent the return bus journey puzzling over. He didn't want to leave it in his pigeon hole, given the degree of unwelcome attention that was getting from Mickey. But where to store it safely until it was time to go home?

In the end he decided to stuff it into the waistband at the back of his trousers, keeping his jacket on in the office so that the bulge wasn't visible. It made the afternoon rather uncomfortable, but he couldn't risk Mickey getting his hands on the package. He tried not to think about the appointment with Miss Honeywell.

When he got home he managed to sneak up to his room without his mother seeing it, and he hid it under his bed behind some old school bags. Then he lay down, feeling exhausted by the day's events, until his mother called him for supper. He sat at the kitchen table, and started to toy with the shepherd's pie on his plate.

"Are you all right, Joseph?"

He looked up into his mother's face. There was concern in her eyes, but also tiredness, a sense of having been worn down by the world. He knew he couldn't add to her worries by telling her all of his problems. Or even his dreams about flying.

"Yes, mum," he said, forcing a small smile.

"Everything all right at work?"

It took a lot of effort for him not to react to that, as an image of Janice Honeywell's stern face flooded into his mind. Instead he just nodded. "Yes, fine, thanks."

"I hope Mr Churchill appreciated the effort you made over the weekend. Going all the way out to his country estate."

"Oh, yes, he's been very kind to me," Joseph mumbled, feeling even more guilty about the lies he had told her.

"Good."

His mother started to eat, apparently satisfied that all was well in the world of her son, and Joseph sat in silent agony, wishing he could tell her the truth. He remembered how she would hold him when he was a little boy, soothing and comforting him, telling him everything was going to be all right. He desperately wanted everything to be all right again, and the need was a pain in his chest that nearly made him gasp.

"What's wrong, Joseph?"

He grabbed his glass and took a gulp of water before answering. "Bit of food, went down the wrong way. I'm all right now."

His mother nodded, and picked up her fork again. *Monmouth would be proud of me*, he thought bitterly. *I've become such an accomplished liar.*

The remainder of the meal passed in silence, and after supper he excused himself and returned to his room. All thoughts of Monmouth's package were now forgotten as he worried about what would happen the next morning at work. Would he be fired? Would he be arrested? How could he prove that he hadn't taken the draft? Perhaps he should have gone to Miss Honeywell as soon as Mickey had threatened him.

The thoughts and regrets went around and around in his head, preventing him from sleeping properly, and when he awoke in the morning, far too early, he felt completely exhausted. But he couldn't stay in bed another second. He washed, dressed, and set off for work.

TWENTY-SEVEN

Well before the appointed time, Joseph sat waiting in the hard chair in the hallway outside the office of Miss Honeywell. She arrived at about ten minutes to eight, and he stood up in greeting, but, after unlocking the door, she bade him to continue waiting, and entered her office alone. Fifteen minutes later he was still waiting.

Then the door opened slightly, and Miss Honeywell beckoned him into her office. She motioned for him to sit down in one of the high-backed visitor's chairs, while she herself returned to her seat behind the desk. She leaned forward, regarding him through her big black glasses, and then picked up the envelope from the blotter in front of her.

"When and how did you remove this draft from the locked desk drawer of Mr Pinborough, Samson?"

Joseph took a deep breath. "I didn't take it from Mr Pinbourough's desk, Miss. As I said yesterday, I've never before seen that draft." To his relief, his voice sounded calm and level. *Just remember, you've done nothing wrong!*

She frowned at him. "Then how do you explain its presence in your pigeonhole?"

"I believe it was put there by Mickey Cooper."

"Did he also fill your name in on the payee line?"

"He must have. It certainly wasn't me."

"So you are saying you believe that the head clerk stole a draft, forged your name on it, and then placed it in your pigeon hole."

"Yes, Miss."

"Why on earth would he do such a thing?"

Joseph sighed. "He told me that he was going to do it to punish me for not paying him his tribute."

"Tribute? What tribute?"

Joseph explained about the traditional tribute paid to the head clerk by new clerks. "But Mickey demanded an extortionate amount from me, because he thinks I'm a toff, and I refused to pay it."

"How much did he want?"

"Twenty-one shillings. It's more than I make in a week."

Miss Honeywell's eyebrows rose at that. "I agree you cannot afford to pay that much. But why didn't you come to me when Cooper first threatened to do this?"

Joseph frowned. "I wish that I had, now. But I suppose I wasn't certain he would carry out his threat. And I didn't want to be a sneak."

"I wish that you had too." She put the draft down on the desk. "Because this puts me in a difficult situation." She folded her hands together on top of the draft. "I want to believe you, Samson. But this is a very serious matter, and as a bank we cannot afford to employ anyone against whom there is even a breath of suspicion of fraudulent activity. I need proof that you are innocent."

Joseph rubbed his forehead. "Why would I do this thing? It doesn't make sense."

"Perhaps because your family has fallen on hard times, and you want to restore yourself to a life of privilege?"

"No, I would never do that!" But how could he prove that he wouldn't? It was just his word, and wouldn't anyone say that? He felt panic rising in his chest, and he thought desperately for something to say in his defence.

"How would someone forge the signatures on the draft,

anyway? It's worthless without the signatures, isn't it?"

Miss Honeywell narrowed her eyes. "Perhaps it was an opportunistic crime, and you didn't think it through beforehand. Perhaps you noticed that Mr Pinbourough had left his desk drawer unlocked when you delivered his post, and the temptation was too much." She sat back in her chair. "In any event, I don't think it's accurate to say that a blank banker's draft is worthless. I've no doubt that there are nefarious characters in the underworld who would pay a considerable sum for such an item. Professional forgers, and the like."

Joseph wiped his hand across his mouth. It wasn't fair to expect him to refute every possible scenario that she came up with. But then he thought of another point. "Why do you think my name was entered in block capitals?"

"I don't know why. You tell me."

"To disguise the writing of the person who did it! If Mickey had written in cursive it would have been obvious that it wasn't my hand."

Miss Honeywell nodded. "That is a good point. But not conclusive. You yourself might have written in block capitals for the same reason."

Joseph shook his head, frustration mounting. "Look, the whole thing is ridiculous! I don't even have a bank account in my name! How could I have paid the draft in?"

Miss Honeywell looked at him sternly. "Joseph, I know this is hard for you, but you must control your temper. Kindly moderate your tone."

"I'm sorry, Miss."

"That's better. Now, what I propose to do is to investigate further. I will interview Mr Cooper, and I will check with the other banks to make sure that what you have said about a bank account is true. I will also compare the handwriting on the draft with some of the written work done by yourself and by Mr Cooper. Until I have concluded my investigations, I believe it is better if you do not come in to work."

Joseph opened his mouth to protest, but she held up her hand, and continued. "You will still be paid, but I cannot take the risk until I am certain that you are innocent. I'm sorry, but that is the way it has to be."

She stood up, and Joseph was obliged to follow suit. "Go home, Samson, and remain there until Friday. I should have reached a conclusion by then. You may come to my office again on Friday at eight in the morning, and I will let you know what my decision is. Good day."

Joseph turned and stumbled out of the office, his thoughts in turmoil. What could he do? If he returned home now, it would cause his mother tremendous worry, and he couldn't do that to her. But what were the other possibilities? Wander the streets all day while she thought he was at work?

He descended the stairs in a daze, and walked out into the street. The morning bustle now seemed to exclude him, because he alone out of all the hurrying people had nowhere to go and nothing to do. He chose a direction at random, and started walking.

TWENTY-EIGHT

After wandering around aimlessly for a while, he remembered that his mother would be at work by now. As long as he went out again well before she was due back, he would in fact be able to go home. So he did so.

Letting himself into the house was a strange feeling. He was never home at this time on a weekday, and the whole atmosphere of the house was unfamiliar. It almost seemed to him that it resented being disturbed from its normal quiet routine by his presence. He tried to dismiss the thought, and climbed the stairs to his bedroom.

Flopping down on the bed, he tried to read, but his thoughts kept returning to his dire work situation, and it was impossible to concentrate. He threw the book down with a sigh, and cast about for something to distract him. He suddenly remembered his meeting with Monmouth the day before, and leaned over and pulled the package out from under his bed. He hefted it in his hand, wondering what was in it. This was clearly no test envelope; there must be something inside that Monmouth badly wanted to get onto Aeropolis. But what?

He shook the package, and it seemed he could hear a

slight clinking sound. He squeezed it here and there, but whatever it contained was obviously well-padded, and felt quite solid. He was dying to know what was in it. Part of him knew it was just a distraction that his mind had seized on, but he didn't care. He started to look carefully at the string binding, trying to work out if it was possible to slip the strings off without disturbing the wax seal, so that he could unfold some of the paper cover.

After about ten minutes of careful manipulation, he managed to get the string on one side slid off, allowing him to start unfolding the paper. He did it very carefully so as not to tear it, trying to remember how it was folded so that he could fold it back again the same way.

Whatever was inside the package was wrapped in some heavy brown sack-cloth. He managed to tease a fold of it outwards until he found an edge. Peering down through the folds, he saw the glint of metal.

By carefully widening the gap he was able to grasp the end of a fat metal tube, which he used to slide the whole thing out into his hand. It was about the size of a cigar tube, but much heavier, made of some dull silver metal. One end appeared to be some sort of cap, about two inches long, with a burred grip at its base. He carefully twisted the grip, and was able to unscrew the cap and remove it. Beneath the cap the end of the tube tapered into a sharp metal spike, with a series of round holes that ran all the way around the tube just below the base of the spike. A ring of wicked barbs encircled the tube above the screw thread that the cap engaged with; it looked as if the removal of the cap allowed them to spring away from the barrel of the tube, so that their ends pointed downwards. Joseph replaced the cap, noticing how it pushed the barbs back against the barrel again.

The other end had a sort of dial on it, with numbered graduations engraved on the tube, and a knurled knob above them. A red line painted on the knob was lined up with the letter S engraved just before the number zero on the dial, which ran up to the number thirty in multiples of five.

Joseph had absolutely no idea what it was. He had hoped

to find something that identified Vanross, some incriminating document, but this meant nothing to him. If he went to Hughes with this, there was no telling what his reaction might be. Joseph might end up making things a lot worse for himself.

There seemed to be about half-a-dozen of the strange tubes in the package, and nothing else. He tightened the cap on the one he had removed, and carefully slid it back into place. He decided not to try re-wrapping the package just yet; there was time to do it before Friday, and perhaps he would need to look at them again, if something occurred to him in the meanwhile. So he replaced the package under his bed as it was.

The opening of the package had been a welcome distraction, but now that it was over the weight of his problems fell heavily on him again, and he sighed miserably. He glanced at his watch. It wasn't even eleven yet. The day stretched out before him, empty and uninviting. What was he going to do with himself?

Even though it was a little early, he decided to go down to the kitchen and see what he could do about lunch. He had just opened the door of the pantry when the telephone rang, and he ran to answer it.

"Hello, this is Joseph Samson speaking."

A male voice replied. "This is the air-to-ground operator on Aeropolis. Please stand by for Miss Hughes."

For a few moments, all Joseph heard was hissing and static. Then there was a click.

"Hello? Joseph, are you there?" Ione's voice made his heart soar. In an instant his mind was back on Aeropolis. He could picture her standing in the marbled hallway of Hughes's apartments, holding the telephone receiver in both hands.

"Hello, Ione," said Joseph. "How are you?"

"Oh Joseph, I'm very well! How are you? I phoned the bank first, and they said you were at home. Are you ill?"

Joseph didn't want Ione to know about his problems at work, it was too embarrassing. The white lie came easily to his lips. "Just a bit under the weather." He managed a small cough. "Should be all right again tomorrow."

"Oh good, glad it's nothing serious. Because I wanted to speak to you about coming back to Aeropolis soon, to see me off."

"See you off?" Joseph's heart sank. "Why, where are you going?"

"I'm sorry to say that Aeropolis is leaving London on Friday. We're heading into Europe. I was hoping you could get away from work for a few hours before then."

"Yes, I think I could manage it. Actually, I have a few days' leave due to me. I could come for more than a few hours if you like. I could stay over again."

"Oh, that would be great! When were you thinking of?"

"Tomorrow might be best."

"Perfect, if you can get permission."

"I'll ring them now and check. But it should be absolutely fine, no doubt about it."

"It's probably better to be sure. Daddy said I can send a ship to pick you up, so I'll make those arrangements, and call you back in an hour or so to confirm it's OK on your end."

"All right, speak to you in an hour."

Joseph rang off, and continued with his lunch preparations. He felt excited to be seeing Ione again, although it was tinged with sadness that she would be leaving soon. But most of all he was glad that he had something to do, so that he didn't have to keep sneaking back into the house after his mother had left for work…

It suddenly hit him. What was he going to tell his mother? She knew that he didn't have any leave due to him. And he couldn't simply disappear overnight. What would he say to her?

By the time Ione called back, he had worked it out. The phone rang, and he answered to hear the operator's voice again. Then Ione came on the line.

"It's all been arranged."

"On my side as well."

"Excellent! Do you know London Air Park?"

"Yes, it's where I went from last time. What's the name of the ship?"

"Oh, I've got it written down here somewhere." There were sounds of paper shuffling in the background. "Here it is! The name is the *Lotus Flower.* "

Joseph was very surprised to hear that. "Oh, I see. Did your father arrange the ship?"

"No, I don't think so! He's far too busy. It must have been Blake. Why?"

"Nothing really. It's just that it's the same ship I travelled on last time. But Blake organised that trip too, so he must have used the same captain."

"I suppose so." Ione didn't sound particularly interested in that line of conversation. "Anyway, if you can be at London Air Park by ten tomorrow, the ship will be waiting. I'll see you shortly afterwards."

"Looking forward to it."

He rang off, feeling both excited and apprehensive at the same time, and ran upstairs to pack. As he laid out his clothes he suddenly remembered the package. With a sinking feeling, he realised wasn't going to have nearly as much time as he had thought he would to decide what to do with it.

Bending down, he slid the package out from under the bed. It was still half-open. He closed it up again roughly, and held it in his hand, thinking about what to do with it.

After a few moments' thought he decided it would be better to take it with him. It wasn't that that he meant to leave it at the drop. Rather, he was just taking care of it. If he did manage to think of a way to show it to Hughes without incriminating himself, he would. And he certainly didn't want to leave it at home, where his mother might find it. The little tubes might even be dangerous. He pushed the packet to the bottom of his suitcase, and closed the lid.

When his mother returned from work, she was surprised to find him already home, but he explained that as he had been asked to accompany Churchill on a business trip to Birmingham the next day, where they would be staying overnight, he had been allowed to leave work early to pack. His mother accepted this with a comment on how much Churchill was coming to rely on him, which made him feel guilty again, and then she started cooking their supper. The evening seemed to drag as much as the day had, but eventually it was time to go to bed. He set his alarm clock even earlier than usual, and turned out the light, thoughts full of Ione and Aeropolis.

TWENTY-NINE

IONE

She was waiting at the passenger terminal from soon after ten, looking out anxiously for Joseph's face in the crowd. As he wasn't on a scheduled flight, she really had no idea of his arrival time, so all she could do was wait, and hope that the captain of the *Lotus Flower* was a reasonably punctual man.

Unfortunately it was nearly noon by the time she saw Joseph, towering over the other passengers as he made his way along the concourse. She stood up, waving frantically, and eventually he spotted her, and made his way over, smiling.

"Hello, Ione," he said. "It's good to see you again."

She grinned at him. "Come on. I've got a surprise for you." She grabbed his hand, and rushed off through the crowds, fairly dragging him along. He laughed good-naturedly, and did his best to keep up.

Before long she had led him to a little cafe overlooking the promenade. She found a table next to the windows which gave a wonderful view out over the promenade, and the deck beyond. Joseph looked at her quizzically.

"This is very nice," he said, gesturing at the cafe around

them. In truth it was rather plain, and half-filled with men in greasy overalls, but it wasn't for the ambiance that Ione had brought him here. She grinned at him.

"Sit down, and look out of the window. Towards the deck."

Joseph obeyed, staring out with a slight frown. Just at that moment, they heard the sudden roar of a high-powered aero engine, and Joseph's eyes widened as he spotted a little plane starting down the runway that bisected the deck area directly in front of them.

"That's a Spitfire!" he said, grinning from ear to ear.

"Yes, that's why we're here. After your little flying adventure the last time you were with us, I thought you'd like to watch the Spitfires taking off and landing, while we have lunch."

Joseph glanced at her, eyes shining. "You're definitely right about that." He turned back to the window, and watched the plane take off and fly away, until it was no longer in sight.

She watched him indulgently, gratified by his happiness. He turned back to face her, smiling contentedly.

"Thank you. It's very thoughtful of you to do this."

She smiled back. "It's my pleasure."

After the waitress had taken their order, a second Spitfire came in for a high-speed landing, and he watched it attentively all the way in, right until it had turned out and lined up next to the other parked Spitfires, and the pilot had killed the engine. She began to realise that she hadn't quite thought through her little plan. It was actually quite annoying to be with someone whose attention could be so completely captured by something else.

At last he turned back to her. "So, have you picked up any more mysterious radio messages?" He grinned as he said it, which annoyed her. It was as if he didn't take her concerns seriously.

"No, I haven't. Although I've only been listening now and again."

He nodded, eyes already wandering back to the runway. She fought down her annoyance, and ploughed on.

"But I *have* been following Thornton again, although he hasn't done anything else suspicious. Still, I'm certain it's him, based on that conversation I overheard."

At this Joseph's attention snapped back to her, and his forehead creased in a frown. "Are you certain that you didn't misunderstand what was said?"

"Of course I am! Why would you even ask that? You weren't there."

"I know, it's just…" He looked very uncomfortable. "I don't think we should jump to any premature conclusions, that's all."

She took a deep breath as she struggled to contain her anger. "Really? OK, let's see what we've got so far. One, the code name I picked up in the radio transmission is Black Rose, which fits Thornton. Two, the radio transmission talked about a failed attempt, and I overheard the pilot saying to Thornton that he had blown his chance."

She glared defiantly at Joseph, but inwardly she suddenly felt less sure. *Is that really all that I have to go on?* The thought made her even more angry. "What other explanation do you have for that?"

Joseph shifted in his seat. "Well, perhaps the code name has absolutely nothing to do with the agent's real name. If you think about it, that actually makes more sense: why would you use a code name that gave away the identity of the person? And as for what the pilot said, maybe it's just a coincidence. Maybe he was speaking about something completely different."

She shook her head slowly. "So you're saying you don't believe me."

Joseph looked anxiously at her. "No, Ione, I'm not saying that! I'm just saying there could be another explanation. The agent could be someone else."

"Who then?"

Joseph threw up his hands. "I don't know! It could be anyone. Blake Vanross, for example."

"Oh, don't be ridiculous! Blake's father worked for my grandfather. There's no-one my father trusts more."

"Well, the code name fits. Blake Vanross. Black Rose."

"You said it didn't make sense for the code name to resemble the real name."

He flushed. "Look, Ione, I don't know who it is! I'm just saying you shouldn't jump to conclusions."

"Keep your voice down, please."

He folded his arms, a sulky look on his face. "Actually, I'm not that hungry any more." He stood up, picking up his suitcase. "I'm going to my room."

She looked at him coolly, toying with a spoon. "How do you think you're going to get into the apartment?"

He flushed an even deeper red, then took a slow breath. "May I please have the key?"

She sat there looking at him for a long moment, savouring his discomfort. He bore it stoically, and suddenly she felt guilty.

"Come on, Joseph. Please sit down, and have lunch with me." But he still hesitated.

"The truth is that you won't be staying in the apartment this time," she said gently. "My father left on a business trip this morning, and he didn't think it would be appropriate for us to be in the apartment together without him there." She smiled slightly. "He's very protective of me. So there's a room reserved for you at the hotel. I'll walk you over there after lunch. But please sit down now."

At last he relented, and resumed his seat just as the food arrived. They ate in silence for a few minutes. Then he wiped his mouth with his napkin, and looked directly at her.

"I'm sorry, Ione. I know it's no excuse for my behaviour, but things have been difficult at work recently."

She nodded. "Oh yes, I'd forgotten that you hadn't been well."

He seemed about to say something, and then stopped himself, smiling sheepishly. "Yes, I suppose that must be it. Not yet completely better." He took a sip of water. An unruly lock of his thick hair fell across his forehead, and he brushed it back.

"I'll forgive you this once." She smiled, and he smiled

back.

After that things were a lot easier between them. They laughed and chatted and she couldn't have said afterwards what it was that they talked about, but the afternoon seemed to go by in the blink of an eye, and the next thing they knew the cafe was closing. They walked out into the golden afternoon and strolled along the promenade towards the hotel, admiring the airships and the cloud vista which surrounded Aeropolis, all painted in gorgeous hues by the lowering sun.

At the hotel she helped Joseph register, signing the bill so that the room would be charged to the Hughes account, and then stood with him in the lobby as the bellhop took his suitcase off to his room.

"You should go with him, rest up. I've got reservations at the jazz club tonight for us."

Joseph grinned. "Really? Wow, that sounds smashing!"

She laughed. English boys said the cutest things sometimes. "I'll be back to pick you up at eight. Meet me down here in the lobby."

He nodded, and turned away to catch up with the bellhop. She watched him go, graceful despite his great height, and then headed back to the apartment.

She spent the time bathing and preparing for the evening, forcing herself to go slowly so as not to be ready too early. She felt slightly guilty about going to the jazz club with Joseph, because she had an ulterior motive for doing so. A little research had uncovered the name of the young pilot that she had seen with Thornton: Jimmy Wales. And further enquiry had established that he was a bit of a jazz buff, who was in the club most nights. So she was hoping to see him, and possibly Thornton, tonight.

She arrived back at the hotel lobby about ten minutes after eight, and Joseph saw her as soon as she walked in, jumping to his feet and coming over to meet her with a broad smile on his face.

"You look very pretty," he said.

"Why, thank you, Mr Samson. And you look very dashing yourself."

It was true; he seemed to have found a reasonably stylish suit somewhere, and his shirt was clean and crisply ironed. She took his arm and strolled out onto the promenade, feeling very grown up and sophisticated.

She had never actually been to the jazz club before, and when she saw the doorman she had a panicky flutter of fear that he wouldn't let them in. But Joseph's height, and probably also her status as a Hughes, meant that the velvet rope was lifted for them with barely a flicker of hesitation. Soon they were seated at a little table with an excellent view of the band. After a few minutes of discordant tuning up, the lights dimmed, and Ella Fitzgerald herself stepped onto the stage, to enthusiastic applause.

Ione used the moment to surreptitiously look around the room, but several minutes of patient scrutiny failed to turn up Jimmy Wales. Stifling her disappointment, she tried to concentrate on the music. Joseph seemed completely entranced by it, and she had to admit that it was very pleasant to be immersed in its mellow glow, the smoky little club a cocoon of smooth sophistication. She settled down to enjoy Ella's voice caressing "Baby, It's Cold Outside".

Minutes or hours later— she couldn't have said which— the spell of the music was broken when something made her look at a man leaning casually against the far wall of the club. As he turned his head towards her she saw that it was Jimmy. Fortunately she was half-facing him, and so was able to keep him in sight without being too obvious about it, by glancing at him from time to time out of the corner of her eye.

Jimmy remained standing there for a number of songs, but when the band took a break, and he turned to go back to his seat, Clive Thornton was suddenly there in front of him. Jimmy's relaxed demeanour vanished, and he drew himself up stiffly as he tried to brush past Thornton, who put an arm up to prevent his passage. The arm was dropped after a furiously whispered exchange, and Jimmy stalked out of the club, followed a few moments later by Thornton.

Ione was on her feet in an instant. She glanced at Joseph's startled face, but after deciding that she didn't have time to explain, she rushed out of the club after Thornton.

Outside the club the promenade was crowded, and she craned her neck to try to catch a glimpse of Thornton or Jimmy, but neither were anywhere to be seen. She hurried along the promenade in random directions, to no avail. There was no sign of the two men anywhere.

With an exclamation of irritation, she turned to go back to the club, and ran straight into Joseph.

"What are you doing, Ione?" His face showed concern and puzzlement.

She stared at him for a moment, trying to gauge what his reaction to the truth might be. "I saw Thornton, together with the pilot he was with when I followed him the first time. I decided to follow them when they left the club."

Joseph's face fell. "So that's what tonight was about. Spying on Thornton again."

She felt a stab of guilt. "Well, not just about that. I wanted to be with you too."

"But you knew they would be at the club."

"I guessed. I wasn't sure."

He sighed, and turned to face the railing, resting his arms on it, and seemed to sag against it.

"Joseph, I'm sorry, I should have told you beforehand." She put her hand on his forearm.

He turned to face her again. "It's just that everything seems to be going wrong for me." He looked so miserable that she felt her heart melt. Without thinking she put her arms around him and hugged him.

THIRTY

JOSEPH

Ione put her arms around him and hugged him tightly, and it felt so wonderful. He hugged her back, feeling her hug become even more fierce, and then his lips found hers, and he was kissing her sweet mouth, and great strong feelings were rushing through his body, and then—

"I-I'm sorry, Joseph," she said, pulling away. "I have a beau. Back home, in New York." Her head was down, and her eyes were shielded by her hair.

"I don't care," he said, bending his head down towards hers, raising her chin with his finger, and it was true, he didn't care, he just wanted that wonderful feeling again—

And then he did care. It was like a fuse, burning slowly through his brain, the idea of her with someone else, some tall blond corn-fed American boy, a quarterback maybe, and suddenly he felt sick with jealousy and he knew he was a complete fool and he pulled away from her, and he turned, and ran.

"Joseph!" she called out after him but he didn't stop and the tears made everything blurry but still he ran.

* * *

After a while the tears stopped, and then he did too. He looked around and saw he was quite close to the hotel. Taking a few moments to compose himself, he walked in and retrieved his key from the front desk. In the hotel room he dropped his jacket on the floor and flopped onto the bed. He curled up into a ball, pulling the counterpane up around him, wishing that the world would just go away and leave him alone. He hugged his misery to himself, trying not to think about Ione and Monmouth and Mickey, and after a while sleep came.

He was woken by a knock on the door. He shook his head groggily, disoriented, his mind a jumble of dark dreams and painful memories. The knocking was insistent, however, so he hoisted himself off the bed with an effort, and crossed the thick pile carpet to open the door.

"Hello, Joseph." The face of Blake Vanross was looking up at him, but there was no trace of his usual soft smile.

Joseph's heart dropped, and he started to close the door, but long before he could do so, Vanross kicked it open wide, and strode in, pushing Joseph back into the room with a hand on the chest as he closed the door behind him.

"What are you doing here?"

"Don't play dumb with me." Vanross's eyes were hard. "Give me the package."

"What package?" Joseph tried as hard as he could to sound innocent. But Vanross narrowed his eyes, and stepped forward again, shoving Joseph hard in the chest again, and making him stagger backwards until he fell onto the bed.

"What part of 'don't play dumb' didn't you understand? Give me the package right now, and I'll think about not hurting you too badly."

Joseph shook his head sullenly. "I don't know what you're talking about."

Vanross grunted in annoyance, and bent down to pick up Joseph's suitcase, which was empty. He threw it onto the bed, then flung open the wardrobe doors, scooping up all of Joseph's clothes and turning to dump them onto the bed next to Joseph. He rummaged roughly through them, seizing almost immediately on the packet which Monmouth had given to Joseph two days previously.

"Why did you open this?" he said, brandishing it in Joseph's face. His voice was low and menacing. "Didn't Monmouth tell you not to tamper with it?"

Joseph nodded.

"So you never meant to deliver it. I thought as much when you didn't make the drop last night. I told Monmouth he was a fool to trust you." Vanross ran a hand through his hair. He pulled one of the metal rods out of the package and looked at it suspiciously. "Have you tampered with these? Do you know what they are?"

Joseph shook his head.

"That's good, I suppose, because they're pretty dangerous." He pulled the chair out from the desk, turned it around, and sat down facing Joseph. "What am I going to do with you?"

Joseph had by now recovered all of his faculties from the grip of sleep, and was thinking the same thing himself. *I'm much bigger than Blake. Why should I let him push me around?* But almost as if he had read Joseph's mind, Vanross reached into his jacket pocket and brought out a dainty silver pearl-handled pistol. He levelled it at Joseph.

"I think you're going to have to come along with me."

The barrel of the gun seemed to be staring at Joseph, like an unblinking black eye. He fought down the fear. "Where are you going?"

"That's on a need-to-know basis. And you don't need to know." He stood up. "This is the way we're going to do this. You'll walk in front of me, and I'll follow behind you. My hand will be in my jacket pocket, holding the gun, pointing at you. It would be a shame to ruin this suit by shooting a hole through it, but you better believe I'll do it if you don't do exactly as I say. Understand?"

Joseph nodded reluctantly. Vanross motioned him to stand up with the gun.

"We're going to walk out of that door, and you're going to turn left, and walk to the elevators, and press the down button. When the car arrives, you're going to get in, and press the button for level one. Not the Deck. Level one. Got it?"

"Yes, I understand. Level one."

"Good. Let's get going." Vanross walked to the door and opened it a crack, peering out. He glanced back at Joseph before opening it a fraction wider and sticking his head out for a quick glance, right and left, before moving back into the room.

"No-one around, which isn't very surprising at seven in the morning." He motioned Joseph towards the door. "Get going. Keep walking, not fast, not slow, don't look back at me. Left to the elevators."

Joseph walked out and turned left, his heart hammering in his chest. His passage on the thick carpet was soundless but he heard the soft click of the door closing behind him. He suddenly got the mad urge to turn around and check that Vanross was actually behind him, that this wasn't all some elaborate practical joke, but he fought it off, trying to stay focused on the seriousness of his situation despite the prevailing sense of unreality. He concentrated on walking at a steady pace, and soon enough came to the lobby. He went up to the lift buttons and pressed the down one. A few seconds later a soft ding announced the arrival of the lift car, and he entered, catching a glimpse of Vanross behind him from the corner of his eye. He pressed the button for level one, the doors slid smoothly closed, and the car set off downwards.

He watched the indicator light moving down through the levels, trying to ignore Vanross's impassive reflection in the shiny inner surfaces of the doors. Desperate fantasies of hitting the emergency stop and spinning around to overpower Vanross flowed through his brain, but they seemed impossibly unlikely. The car slowed to a halt, and the doors slid open.

Vanross stepped forward, placing his left hand over the door edge to keep it open, while pressing the gun against Joseph's back. "Move forward slowly." As Joseph complied,

Vanross peered around the edge of the doorframe, but there didn't seem to be anyone about. He relaxed visibly, removing the gun from his jacket pocket and motioning Joseph forward with it. "Over there, to that door."

Joseph looked for the door, and spotted a door-sized outline in the dark wood wall panelling on the other side of the lobby. As he approached it, Vanross darted forward, removing a key from his pocket, and unlocked the door, which was attached to a section of the wall panel, and opened it inwards. He stood aside and motioned for Joseph to go in.

It was pitch dark inside. When Joseph heard the door close behind him, he felt a moment of panic, but there was a click as Vanross operated a light switch, and a dim bulb in a frosted glass and wire cage illuminated the space in front of him.

They were on a landing at the top of a stairwell, with white-painted walls and and a flight of metal stairs leading down into darkness. Vanross gestured impatiently with the gun.

"Keep going."

Joseph turned and began to descend the stairs.

THIRTY-ONE

At first the stairway led ever further down, with no doors in the walls of the stairwell. But after the third or fourth landing, Joseph could see through the railing that the landing below him had a doorway leading out into some other part of Aeropolis.

It's now or never. He threw himself down the intervening stairs, taking them two or even three at a time, careening precariously around the landing, using the hand rail to keep himself upright, and in a few moments he had grabbed the handle and flung the door open.

Vanross was cursing under his breath and clattering down the stairs behind him, but Joseph didn't even risk a quick glance before running through the door.

He found himself on a high catwalk, constructed of metal gridwork, and suspended from the ceiling by long bars. As he ran the catwalk bounced and moved under his feet, making him feel uneasy, and the air was hazy with steam and filled with the noise of machinery.

Ahead he could see a maze of catwalks and ladders leading over, under and through huge machinery, much of which was obscured by shifting clouds of steam. It was difficult to see a clear path anywhere, and the whine and clatter of the machines, and the insistent hissing and roaring of the steam pipes and boilers, made it hard to think. When he came to a junction, he turned at random onto another catwalk, and ran headlong down it.

But Vanross evidently knew his way around a lot better than Joseph did. His head suddenly poked up at the end of the catwalk in front of Joseph, who skidded to a halt. Vanross vaulted up the stairs and started running down the catwalk towards a transfixed Joseph.

There was a flight of stairs to Joseph's right, leading down into a cloud of steam. Forcing himself to move, Joseph launched himself down the stairs, his feet clattering on the open grid-work as he took them two and three at a time. At the bottom was a grid platform, surrounding a huge boiler: Joseph could feel the heat of it on his face, and the prickly feeling of sweat breaking out. He ran to the right around the giant globe of the boiler, dodging pipes and sudden bursts of steam.

Once he had gone some way around the boiler, he risked a glance backwards. Vanross was nowhere in sight. He slowed down, and descended a stairway to another grid platform that encircled the boiler on a lower level. There, a few paces from the bottom of the stairs, Joseph spotted a little hut, with a light burning inside.

He dashed towards it, hoping to find a workman inside, but it was empty apart from a kettle, some mugs and boxes of teabags, and a metal toolbox. Quelling his disappointment, Joseph opened the tool box and rummaged around inside.

It mostly contained bits of wire and other junk, but there were some screwdrivers. Joseph picked the newest-looking one, with the sharpest blade.

At that moment he felt a discordant vibration through the steel grid floor. Peering out of the hut's little window, he saw Vanross heading towards him, walking cautiously. Joseph ducked under the little counter next to the door of the hut, and hugged his knees, trying to make himself as small as possible.

The tension was unbearable, the desire to jump up and run again almost overwhelming. Fear caught in his throat. *I'm not brave enough for this!*

Vanross's footsteps shook the grid as he approached, slow and measured. Joseph held his breath, clenching his fists until the nails bit painfully into his palms. His arms shook from muscular tension, knuckles brushing the walls of the hut.

There was a pause in the rhythm of the footsteps, a long moment of excruciating fear, as Joseph waited to be discovered, every nerve straining. He squeezed his eyes shut, pressing his fists against the walls. The fear was overwhelming, unrelenting. *I wish I was brave!*

As those words flashed through his mind, he suddenly remembered a conversation he'd had with his father, years earlier. I wish I was brave like you, Dad, he had said. Then I wouldn't be afraid of anything.

His father had smiled at him, shaking his head. Being brave doesn't mean being fearless, Joseph. It means doing what you have to do, even if you are afraid.

Being terrified, but still doing what you have to do. He nodded to himself. He didn't need the fear to go away. He just had to stop it from making him run. He looked at the fear inside him then, and knew it was just a feeling, something he could ignore if he wanted to. He remained still.

Then the footsteps resumed, becoming fainter, as Vanross moved on past the hut. After a few moments the vibrations through the grid stopped altogether.

Joseph let out his breath slowly, and then took a great shuddering gulp of air into his oxygen-starved lungs. He forced his knotted muscles to relax, and rose slowly to his feet on shaky legs.

Bending to retrieve the screwdriver, he then peered carefully out of the door, but there was no sign of his pursuer. Making his way back to the stairway, he descended yet another flight of stairs.

He came out onto a long gallery that ran off into the distance in both directions. He looked from one side to the other, unsure of which way to proceed. Choosing right at random, he set off again cautiously, every sense straining for signs of Vanross.

The steam-laden air meant that visibility was only fifty yards or so. As he walked along, he saw a dark shape materialising at the limit of his vision. Joseph could not make out whether it was Vanross or not. But the figure was motionless, so he decided to move forward cautiously.

A few more steps revealed it to be a workman, who was bent over a control panel. Joseph's heart soared, and he broke into a run, trying to attract the man's attention by yelling out.

The man didn't seem to hear him, and as Joseph got nearer, he saw that the man wore what looked like headphones over his ears. *Probably can't hear me. I'll have to tap him on the shoulder.*

Joseph was about twenty yards away, and thinking about what he would say to the man, when he suddenly felt strong fingers closing around his ankle. He tripped and lost his balance, falling headlong to the floor. His grip on the screwdriver was broken, and it clattered away and fell off the edge of the catwalk.

Looking down through the floor grid, he saw Vanross on the gallery below. He had reached up through the railings to grab Joseph's ankle with his left hand, and with his right he was reaching for Joseph's right arm. Joseph screamed and grabbed onto the grid-work, but he was not strong enough to resist Vanross. Slowly but inexorably he was being dragged over the edge.

Once Vanross had Joseph's legs dangling he wrapped his arms around them and simply used his bodyweight to pull Joseph downwards. No matter how tightly Joseph squeezed his fingers, they were slowly but surely pulled open by the terrible strain. Finally his grip gave way, fingernails tearing painfully against the sharp metal of the grid. The last thing he saw before falling over the edge was the workman, still engrossed in his task, and oblivious to his surroundings.

Joseph managed to maintain his footing as he fell to the

grid below, but Vanross was ready for him, and grabbed him from behind with an arm around the neck. Joseph bucked and struggled against his captor, flinging his arm backwards to connect with Vanross's crotch.

Unfortunately Vanross had anticipated his move, rotating his own hips at the same time. Joseph's arm crashed harmlessly into Vanross's thigh.

"I wouldn't try that again if I were you," Vanross hissed in his ear. To emphasise his words, he jabbed the point of something sharp into Joseph's side, just below the ribs. Joseph felt it pierce his skin through the cloth of his jacket and shirt. He slipped his left hand up under his clothing to the spot. It was tender to the touch, and he could feel a small cut. It felt wet.

He stabbed me. I'm bleeding. The shock made Joseph feel dizzy, and he staggered against Vanross, who struggled to hold him upright.

"Easy, now. I'm not going to hurt you again, so long as you do as I say. Do you understand?"

Joseph nodded. He felt the fight go out of him. He had done what he could; it was up to the others to find him and rescue him now. He just had to survive.

"Good boy," said Vanross, releasing his grip. "Just walk ahead of me, I'll tell you where to go. Remember, I've still got the knife." He prodded Joseph in the back with it, not hard, but enough that Joseph knew it was there. With a stab of fear in his heart, Joseph set off down the gangway.

He hoped that they would run across more workmen as they made their way back to the stairwell, but either Vanross knew how to avoid people, or Joseph was just unlucky. As they entered the stairwell again, and resumed their downward progress, Joseph felt his heart sink further with every step.

Suddenly there was a loud clanging and clattering noise overhead, further up the stairwell. Joseph's heart leaped.

Someone must be up there! He stopped and turned back, trying to see up the centre of the stairwell. But Vanross gave him a straight-armed shove. "Get moving, Samson."

The words were said low and through gritted teeth. Joseph shook his head. He took a deep breath, and started to scream at the top of his lungs.

"HELP! PLEASE HELP ME! CALL SECURITY! I NEED HELP!"

Vanross swore at him, and charged down the stairs, hitting Joseph full in the chest with his shoulder. Joseph felt his balance going. He clutched desperately at the bannister, but it was just out of reach, and his fingers closed on empty air. He fell backwards down the stairs. The terrible feeling of falling lasted only a moment, and then a tremendous impact on his back knocked the wind out of him, followed immediately by a hard blow to the back of his head. Stars flashed in the blackness that overwhelmed his vision, and then he knew no more.

THIRTY-TWO

IONE

She woke early, and lay in bed, feeling miserable. She hadn't meant to lead Joseph on, her hug had just been the action of a friend. Hadn't it? He was very attractive, there was no doubt about that, but that didn't mean she couldn't just be friends with him. Or maybe it did, for him. She hadn't known that he liked her in that way, and perhaps he wouldn't settle for anything else. In which case she had just lost a friend.

After a while she became annoyed with herself for wallowing in self-pity, and she got up and had breakfast whilst deciding what to do. She ended up phoning the hotel to ask Joseph to meet her for lunch at the Glass House, but the the hotel front desk reported that there was no reply from his room, which was odd, as it was only eight. But perhaps he had gone down for breakfast, so she left a message asking him to call her back.

By the time she was washed and dressed it was near nine o'clock, and there was still no word from Joseph, and when she phoned back, still no reply from his room. She hoped that he hadn't returned to London.

Ione was not the sort of girl to sit around waiting for things to happen, so she decided to try tailing Clive Thornton again. There was clearly something odd going on with this Jimmy Wales. Or perhaps she should just confront Thornton and see what his reaction was.

She made her way down to Security HQ, but was told that Thornton had not yet reported in for the day. Frowning in irritation, she wondered where he could be. Then a thought occurred to her, and she left the HQ and made her way back down to the pilots' quarters.

As she approached the door to Jimmy Wales's room, she saw that her instinct had been correct: Thornton was standing outside, facing the open doorway. He seemed oblivious to anything other than the inside of the room, so she moved closer. This brought Jimmy himself into view, standing with his body partly shielded by the half-open door.

"I mean it, Clive," he said. "Go away, and don't come back. Ever." He held himself rigidly, tension evident in every line of his body, and his fingers were white where they gripped the door.

Thornton stepped forward, stopping on the threshold, and looked at the other man imploringly.

"Please, James. Don't do this," he said, his voice thick with emotion. But Jimmy simply stared at him, his face hard as stone, mouth set in a thin line. Just as Ione got the first inkling that she might not have an entire understanding of what was going on in front of her, Thornton did the most extraordinary thing.

He leaned forward, grabbed Jimmy's face in both hands, and kissed him full on the lips.

For a moment Jimmy stood motionless. Then he jerked his head back and straight-armed Thornton in the chest, who staggered backwards into the hall. Jimmy closed the door with a slam. Ione heard the sound of bolts being shot home.

Thornton continued looking at the door with a dazed expression on his face. After a few moments, he turned away, and did a double-take as he saw her.

"Ione! What are you doing here?" He drew himself up to

his full height and adjusted his cap, his normal humourless expression beginning to reassert itself.

She narrowed her eyes at him. "I might ask you the same question."

"Me? Oh, I was just visiting... an old friend."

"Oh really? Do you kiss all of your old friends, or just the ones you're conspiring with?"

Thornton stared at her, open-mouthed, while a range of emotions vied for dominance on his face. Anger, fear, and confusion traced their paths where normally nothing but sourness showed. But then they all faded away, to be replaced by a stony blankness.

"I don't know what you are talking about."

Ione shook her head angrily. "Fine. I'll just go and tell my father."

Fear returned to Thornton's face. "Tell him what, exactly?"

"That you've been sneaking around with this Jimmy Wales, conspiring with Storm Tendency to... do something bad to him!" Thornton looked utterly perplexed as she said this, but she plunged on regardless. "And also that you kissed him, for some reason..." She tailed off, uncertain of her ground, but Thornton's face had darkened.

"You won't do that."

She felt a sudden stab of fear. She was alone in the corridor with him; she knew he had already been involved in something which involved trying to harm her father; what if he kidnapped her? Dragged her off somewhere and... hurt her?

"Don't you touch me, or I'll scream!"

"What?" Thornton looked at her as if she were mad. "I'm not going to do anything to you." He sighed, and removed his cap, running his fingers through his hair. "Look, can we please talk about this? I don't understand half the things you're saying, and I think you may have the wrong idea about me and James. Let's go to my office."

Ione decided that his office was probably a safer place to be, so she nodded, and the two of them walked in silence to

Security HQ. Once there, Thornton led the way into his office, closing the door, and sat down behind his desk. She took a seat in one of the guest chairs.

"So what's this business about Storm Tangent, or whatever it is you said? A threat to your father is something I need to know about, as head of security."

Ione frowned. "So you are saying you haven't heard of Storm Tendency, or Black Rose?"

Thornton looked at her completely blankly. "No, sorry. Why, should I have?"

If he was lying, he was very convincing. Ione scrambled onto safer ground. "Well, you can't deny that you kissed Jimmy. I saw that with my own eyes!"

"Ah." Thornton pursed his lips, and clasped his hands together on the desk in front of him, squeezing them into each other. "No, I suppose I cannot deny that." He took a deep breath, looking at the wall behind Ione, and then turned his gaze upon her.

"Well? Why did you do it? What's going on with you two?"

Thornton bit his lip, and rubbed his forehead with a finger. "I rather think that's private, to be honest. Anyway, I doubt you would understand. It's… a delicate subject, and something better suited to grownup discussion."

"Oh really? Do you mean like my father?"

Thornton sat up straight at that, alarm on his face. "Now, Ione, I'd really rather that your father didn't know about— what you saw."

"Why?"

He sighed. "You really wouldn't understand. It's very complicated."

"Try me."

He looked at her with an anguished expression. "I can't."

She stood up. "Pity. Ah well, I suppose I'll have to tell my father then. I really can't decide whether or not to keep your little secret unless I understand it, and since you can't explain it—"

"All right!" Thornton was on his feet. "All right, I'll explain it. Sit down, please." He resumed his own seat with a resigned sigh. Ione sat down as well, and looked at him expectantly. But Thornton found a spot on the wall behind her to fix his attention on when he began to speak.

"As you know, most men find a woman, get married, and have children." He cleared his throat. "But some men don't want that." He rubbed his forehead, looking very uncomfortable. "Some men prefer... that is, they like being with... other men."

She frowned. "You mean, as friends? But most men like being friends with other men. They go to football games and stuff."

Thornton shook his head. "No, I don't mean as friends. I mean... as lovers." He almost whispered it, dropping his gaze, and pinching the bridge of his nose between forefinger and thumb.

Ione was thunderstruck. "You mean, you and Jimmy... he is... your *boyfriend?*" It was hard to get her head around the idea.

Thornton nodded. "Well, he was my boyfriend. I did something stupid, and now he won't see me anymore. As you must have witnessed." He looked sad.

Questions were flooding through Ione's mind. She had a vague idea of the mechanics of sex, from whispered conversations in the school dorm after lights-out, but she just couldn't imagine what two men would do together...

She shook her head. There was a lot to think about, clearly, but in the meantime, it was obvious that she had completely misread the relationship between Thornton and Jimmy. Although who could blame her? How could she possibly have imagined such a thing?

Thornton was looking directly at her again. "Ione, the reason why you have never heard of this... type of love before today, is because most people think it is very wrong, and it is not spoken of in polite company." He rubbed his chin. "If your father were to find out about this, I don't know how he would react. I might lose my position, and I don't want that to happen."

Ione frowned. "Daddy wouldn't fire you just because you

love someone."

"I would hope not. But it's just not as simple as that. When you are older you may come to realise that such things can become quite complex. I really don't want to take the chance. Can you understand that?"

Ione nodded. "I think so. But I don't want to lie to my father."

"I understand that, of course, and I'm not asking you to lie. If he asks you directly, then you must tell him the truth. I'm only asking you not to volunteer the information."

There was a fine line there, she felt. But it seemed that for the moment there was nothing to be gained by antagonising Thornton. "All right. I won't tell him if he doesn't ask."

Thornton looked hugely relieved. "Thank you." He almost smiled, for a moment. Then he became serious again.

"Now, tell me about this other business, with the strange names you mentioned."

Ione took a deep breath, and told the story of the intercepted transmissions, her thought processes, and her conversations with Joseph. Thornton listened carefully, asking questions from time to time to clarify things. When she had finished he sat back in his chair, fingers steepled before him.

"The content of the interception is disturbing, and the timing is, as you say, suspicious. Now it could be coincidental, or the entire thing may have an entirely innocent explanation, some type of joke perhaps." He held up his hand as she drew breath, ready to burst out again. "Now I'm not saying I won't do anything about it, so calm down. But we do need to take all possibilities into account. And obviously it is to be hoped that it is nothing to worry about. Anyway, the first thing I want to do is speak to the head of communications about setting up twenty-four hour monitoring of that frequency." He stood up. "I'd better do it in person. Will you wait here? I'll have tea brought in if you like."

Ione nodded, and Thornton left the office. She sat back in the chair. It was good that someone was finally taking her seriously, but she was back to square one with the identity of Black Rose, and she was frustrated that Thornton was now doing things while she was just waiting around. She got up and opened the office door, looking out into a large open-plan room with several desks set in neat rows. Most of them were unoccupied, but many were piled with manila folders and trays of paperwork. At the front of the office, facing the entrance, was a long wooden counter. The duty officer was sitting behind it on a high stool, reading a newspaper.

She was just about to go back into Thornton's office when she spotted a familiar face. It was the apprentice that Joseph was friendly with. *What was his name?* Harry, maybe. She watched him go up to the duty officer, and begin an earnest conversation.

Some intuition made her go closer. Harry was trying to explain something, an urgent tone in his voice. The duty officer was openly skeptical, his attention mostly still on his newspaper.

"How much longer are you going to keep me waiting?" asked Harry, with an edge in his voice. "I've been here for ages!"

The duty officer lowered his newspaper with a sigh. "What did you want to report again?"

Harry rolled his eyes. "I told you already, he was screaming blue murder! 'Help, help,' he was saying, and 'call Security'. You've got to send someone to have a look." Harry drummed his fingers on the counter top.

The duty officer raised an eyebrow at this. "I don't have to do anything, young man. However, a report will be filed, and if thought necessary, it will be investigated in due course."

Harry threw up his hands. "In due course? He ain't going to be around long enough for due course, and that's a fact!"

"What's going on here?" said Ione. The duty officer turned to her in annoyance, but then became more respectful when he recognised her. Harry seemed to recognise her as well, turning his earnest, pleading expression onto her.

"Miss Hughes! Maybe you can help me, get Mr Hughes to do something."

"Do something about what?"

"Some wild goose chase, no doubt," said the duty officer, rolling his eyes.

Harry turned on him. "It's not!" He faced Ione again. "I heard it, miss, with my own ears. He was crying out for help!"

"Where was this?"

"In the emergency stairwell. I was s'posed to paint the bannisters, and I'd just started setting up when I heard it. Bloodcurdling, it was."

The duty officer snorted. "So you came running up here, instead of doing your work. I wonder why that was?"

Harry glared at him. "He was shouting for help, and for Security! So I came here, yes. That's what you are, aren't you? It does say Security on the door, doesn't it?"

"It does," replied the duty officer coldly, "and as I have said, you may consider the incident reported, and it will be investigated in due course."

Harry's eyebrows suddenly shot up, and he turned back to Ione. "You know, miss, I've just realised something. The voice in the stairwell. It was Joseph's!"

Ione's blood ran cold. "What do you mean? Tell me everything that happened."

Harry gulped. "It was like I said, miss. The guv'nor told me to paint the bannisters, so I went in at the top, on Level One. I was just carryin' the paint tins in when it happened. I knocked a paint tray down the stairs. Made a heck of a racket. When it stopped falling, that's when I heard it. A voice, screaming out for help."

"And you're sure it was Joseph's?"

Harry nodded. "Pretty sure, miss. I thought at the time there was something familiar about it, but I was thinking it must be one of my own crew, you know? Then when I saw you, I made the connection. Remembered Joseph."

She turned to the duty officer. "I need to make a telephone call."

He shrugged, and pushed his desk instrument over to her. She quickly dialled the number of the hotel.

"May I speak with Joseph Samson, please? He's in room 329."

There was a long pause. Then the front desk clerk came back on the line. "I'm afraid there's no answer from that room, miss."

"He hasn't checked out, has he?"

"No, miss, that room is still listed as occupied."

"Thank you." She rang off, and turned to Harry. "It could have been Joseph. I haven't been able to contact him all morning. You must take me to this stairwell."

The duty officer looked alarmed. "If there really is a threat, Miss Hughes, is it wise to do that? Why don't you wait here while I contact Commander Thornton?"

Ione looked at him, annoyed by his sudden show of concern. "Maybe he'll respond more quickly when you tell him I've gone there already."

She turned to Harry. "Come on, then. Let's go."

THIRTY-THREE

JOSEPH

He opened his eyes. Spots swam in his vision, and he shook his head to clear them. This turned out to be a mistake. Pain exploded behind his eyes, and he gasped, closing them. When the pain had receded to a dull ache, he tried opening them again. The spots were still there. They were dark against a grey background, and as he watched, another one appeared, and then another. He suddenly realised they were drops of blood. His blood. His head was hanging down, his chin against his chest, and he could feel the blood running down his right temple, and see it dropping onto the floor.

He was sitting in a steel chair, with his hands tied behind his back. His body was slumped forward, and the rope was biting painfully into his wrists. He leaned back to relieve the strain.

"Ah, Sleeping Beauty awakes." It was Vanross's voice, but Joseph couldn't see him. There was a curved wall in front of him that seemed to be covered in some type of silver-painted fabric, and to the left he could see a curved metal girder running from floor to ceiling.

Footsteps. Vanross appeared in his field of view, staring at him balefully.

"That wasn't a very smart thing to do, now was it? You could have come along with me quietly, and witnessed my greatest triumph in relative freedom and comfort. But instead you had to try to be a hero. So now you're immobilised, and in pain. And you're going to be closer to the action than you want to be."

Joseph shook his head, slowly and carefully. "What are you talking about?" His voice was a croak.

"I'm talking about these." Vanross produced the package with a flourish, and extracted one of the metal tubes. "Beautiful piece of work, isn't it?" He held it up as though it were an object of fine art, turning it this way and that. "Monmouth gets one of his mad German engineers to make them."

"What is it?"

Vanross unscrewed the cap, revealing the wicked spike. "Well, it's pretty simple. This spike is made to penetrate the envelope of an airship, and these barbs then prevent it from falling out again. You set the timer delay by turning this knob here, and then the timer counts down."

"Until what?"

"Until detonation, of course! This will make a small but hot explosion, which in turn will detonate the lifting gas. Boom! Bye-bye airship." He bared his teeth in a feral smile.

Joseph frowned. "What airship? H-1?"

"Nope, not H-1. Something much, much bigger."

"I don't know what you are talking about." Joseph found it hard to concentrate on what Vanross was saying.

Vanross turned to the fabric-covered wall. "Aeropolis is nothing but a giant airship, isn't she? Now that over there is the envelope of one of her lifting cells!"

Joseph wished he could rub his aching head. "So you're going to try to blow up Aeropolis?"

"Oh, yes." Vanross stared at the detonator in his hand with a strange expression on his face. "Indeed I am." His voice had dropped to a whisper. "Yes, sirree. Gonna blow it sky-high."

A cold fear settled in Joseph's stomach as he stared at Vanross. The man sounded deranged. But something nagged at him, something that didn't make sense. He tried to concentrate on it, but his head hurt distractingly, and the thought was elusive. He closed his eyes, and concentrated.

Then it burst into his mind.

"That's not going to work. Aeropolis is filled with helium, not hydrogen. Helium doesn't burn or explode." Relief flooded through him. Vanross obviously was deranged, if he had forgotten that elementary fact.

But Vanross simply smiled knowingly. "What makes you think that Aeropolis is filled with helium?"

Joseph frowned. "Well, Monmouth told me—" He stopped as a sick realisation hit him.

Vanross smiled gloatingly. "Yes, Monmouth told you. But, like a lot of things he said to you, it was a lie. Aeropolis *is* filled with hydrogen, and she'll go up like a Roman candle." He laughed, and the sound was dreadful, maniacal.

Joseph stared at him, as the worst fear he had ever known settled on him like a black cloud, snuffing out all hope and life. *I'm going to die, and so is everyone else on Aeropolis.*

THIRTY-FOUR

IONE

As they made their way towards the stairwell, Ione began to have second thoughts about her bravado, but she couldn't turn around now, not in front of Harry, who was forging ahead eagerly, and looking back over his shoulder periodically to be sure that she was following.

They entered the stairwell, and began to descend. "Where does this lead to?" she asked.

"It goes right the way down through all the decks. Ends up between the outer and inner lifting cells."

She frowned. Maybe whoever had kidnapped Joseph— probably Black Rose— was intending to do something to the lifting cells. Cause a gas leak, maybe, so that Aeropolis would have to be evacuated. "We should go down there."

Harry looked at her uncertainly. "It's a long way down, miss."

"Let's get going, then." She pushed past him and began to clatter down the stairs as fast as her legs could move.

The succession of identical flights of stairs seemed endless, and after a while Ione began to feel as if she were in some nightmare, where the stairs did in fact go on forever, and she felt slightly panicky. She rushed on faster, taking the stairs two at a time, and racing around each landing to look down the stairs at the next flight, hoping against hope it would be the last.

Eventually it was. They had reached the bottom. Harry cautiously opened the door that led out of the stairwell. "No-one there," he said, and moved quietly through it. She followed him into a curved corridor. The inner wall was covered in a silvery fabric. "That's the inner lifting cell ring," said Harry.

Ione nodded, looking to the left and right, trying to decide which way to go. "I suppose we'd cover more ground if we split up. But if you see or hear anything, turn around and come find me, OK?"

Harry nodded, and set off to the left, as she started walking to the right. After about fifty yards, she came to an opening in the right-hand wall. It was the mouth of a short passageway, at the end of which was another corridor running at right angles to it. She walked along it cautiously, emerging into the second corridor facing another fabric-covered wall, which seemed to bulge outwards. This time she turned left, and walked along the new corridor, which was less tightly curved, trying to see as far ahead as possible.

Presently she saw what looked like a steel chair, with a dark figure seated upon it. She stopped, then crept forward as silently as she could, hugging the inside wall. But as she got closer, she saw that what had looked like a person was actually just a pile of paint-stained drop cloths. There were some tins of paint, and a couple of boxes of paint rollers, rags, thinners, and small paintbrushes standing next to the chair.

Leaning against the chair was a long metal rod, with a grip on one end. She inspected it more closely. It was hollow, with a fitting on the other end that would take a paint roller. By picking it up and hefting it she discovered that its weight was not much more than that of a sabre. It felt good in her hand, and she decided to carry it. She felt a little better now that she was armed, even if it was only with a rod.

She resumed her progress along the curved corridor, and soon she heard voices up ahead. Moving ahead more cautiously, she tried to make out what they were saying. Her heart leapt when she recognised Joseph's voice, but a moment later she was stunned to hear Blake's voice as well. She listened carefully, but there was no doubt about it.

What in the world is Blake doing here with Joseph? Have they both been kidnapped by Black Rose? But she hadn't heard a third voice. She stopped, crouching down, and concentrated on what was being said.

"Look, I can help you. We could do this thing together." Joseph's voice sounded strained, and there was a wheedling tone in it that made her uncomfortable. But what thing was he talking about?

"Don't need any help, thanks." Blake's tone was clipped, and slightly derisive. "Even if there was something you could do, why would I trust you?"

Ione frowned. Why was Blake speaking so oddly to Joseph? She listened carefully to Joseph's reply.

"You can trust me if you're working against Howard Hughes, because I hate him!"

Ione had to stifle a gasp. What on earth was going on? Why would Joseph say such a thing?

"Oh, you hate him, do you?" Blake's reply was almost bored. "I suppose you're going to tell me why, too."

"He was rude to me." Joseph's tone was defensive.

Blake gave a mocking laugh. "Lord have mercy! *Rude* to you? Say it isn't so. No wonder you *hate* him." There was a pause, and then Blake's voice continued. "So tell me, Joseph, do you think everyone that Howard has been rude to hates him? Hell, is there even anyone he *hasn't* been rude to?"

The shock of what she had heard was wearing off, and in its place, anger was building as she listened to the disrespectful way the two of them were speaking about her father.

"Come on, Joseph," he continued, his tone becoming more and more mocking. "Haven't you got anything else to tell me, to show me how much you hate Howard? How you've been itching to join a plot against him? How you're just the man for the job? Hmm? Come on. Don't be so modest!"

Ione was seething as she waited for Joseph's reply. What would he say to that?

When it came, it was an angry shout. "You know damn well why I hate Hughes. He killed my father!"

It was too much for Ione. She got to her feet in a blaze of anger and charged around the corner, screaming like a madwoman.

THIRTY-FIVE

JOSEPH

"Joseph Samson, that is a lie! My father has never killed anyone! How could you say such a thing?"

Joseph looked up in astonishment as Ione came charging around the curve of the corridor, face red with fury, brandishing some sort of metal rod. But when she saw him, she pulled up short, confusion and concern replacing the anger on her face as she took in the scene. "What is going on here?"

"Well, if it isn't the brave Miss Hughes. Come to rescue your boyfriend?"

Ione narrowed her eyes at that, and seemed about to reply. But Vanross continued, turning to face Joseph. "She's right, you know." There was sardonic amusement in his voice. "Howard Hughes had nothing to do with the death of your father."

"But Monmouth said—" Joseph stopped himself as he remembered Vanross's words from earlier. *Everything Monmouth told me was a lie.* Vanross looked at him knowingly.

"Yes, by golly, I do believe he's starting to learn. Very good, Joseph." He clapped his hands mockingly. Then he turned to Ione. "Anyway, Miss Hughes, you are most welcome to join Joseph. I'll find you another chair, don't you worry." He pulled the gun from his pocket, and took a step towards her.

Ione turned to face him, almost casually, but as she did so her movement flowed into something that was obviously well-practiced, and she ended up in a narrow stance facing Vanross, her rod held lightly but steadily, pointed at his chest.

"I'm going to have to ask you to put that thing down," said Vanross, but almost before he had finished speaking, she darted forward in stance, the rod a blur as she brought it down onto the gun hand. There was a dull thump as it impacted with flesh, and then the gun clattered to the floor. Vanross jumped back with an exclamation of pain, wringing his hand. Ione stepped forward coolly and picked up the gun.

"You better give that to me, little girl, before you hurt yourself with it." Vanross's voice was full of bravado, but Ione was having none of it.

"Get back," she said, waving the gun in his general direction. "I need to speak to Joseph about something."

She turned to face him, eyes blazing, and he felt himself curling up under the heat of her gaze like a leaf in a bonfire. But her words, when they came, were icy.

"Why were you trying to help him?" She cast a contemptuous glance at Vanross. "Why did you say that you hated my father?"

"Ione, listen to me. He's trying to blow up Aeropolis!" This produced a look of shock from her, and so he pressed on. "I was trying to stop him! I just said that I hated your father because I was trying to get him to trust me, so that he would untie me! I was pretending to go along with him so that I could turn on him later, and stop what he's doing. He's a monster. Ione, you've got to believe me!"

She frowned. "I want to, Joseph, I really do. But I need to be absolutely sure that you have nothing to do with this."

"I don't. Please believe me, I don't! I'm only trying to help."

Vanross cleared his throat. "Is that so, Joseph? Perhaps you can explain to Miss Hughes how it was that you brought these on board, then." He held up the package of detonators.

"What are those things?"

"Care to explain, Joseph?" Vanross paused meaningfully, a gloating smile on his face. "Thought not. Guess I'll have to do it then. These little old boys, Miss Hughes, are detonators. When you push them through the skin of an airship, they produce a timed explosion, which ignites the lifting gas."

Ione's face went white. "You meant to use those in the lifting cells." Vanross nodded. She turned to Joseph. "Is this true, what he's saying? That you brought them on board?"

Joseph stared at her, speechless. But his lack of reply was condemnation enough. She shook her head slowly, tears filling her eyes.

"How could you? How could you do this to me? To us?"

"That ain't the half of it, sweetheart. He's being playing you for a fool since day one. Don't know how Monmouth found him, but he sure can pick them."

"You're working for Robert Monmouth?" She put her hand over her mouth. "Daddy was right all along! The ZA *do* want to destroy Aeropolis."

Joseph stared at her, his mind racing through denials and reassurances, but they sounded so false and trite to his own ear that his voice was stilled, and he felt helpless. All he could do was stare into her eyes, shaking his head slowly.

He became aware that Vanross had taken advantage of Ione's distress to move silently up behind her. His warning cry died on his lips as Vanross pounced, wrapping his arms around Ione from behind, trapping her gun arm against her side with a whoop of triumph.

"You bet we wanna destroy Aeropolis, little lady, and we're gonna do it too!" Vanross reached down with his right hand and grasped the silver pistol, wrenching it free from Ione's grasp, and then he stepped back, grinning in triumph. Ione regarded him with dull eyes. Something inside her seemed to have broken. He steered her to another metal chair, sat her down, and bound her wrists behind her back. She offered no resistance.

Seeing this made Joseph even more determined to escape, and he struggled against his own bonds. He pulled and strained, flexing his arms and tightening his shoulder muscles, but the knots were tight, without the slightest give. After a few minutes he slumped back in his chair, defeated both physically and mentally.

Vanross was busily at work with the detonators. He unscrewed the cap on each one, then carefully turned the knurled knob on the base, squinting to line up the indicator lines. Once he had all of them done, he started to insert them into the fabric of the cell envelope. Two went into the fabric wall directly in front of Joseph and Ione, widely spaced, two more went into the wall beyond the girder to the left, and Monmouth took the final two off to the right, returning after a few moments empty-handed, and whistling a cheerful tune.

Joseph regarded him sullenly. He desperately wanted to say something to show that Vanross hadn't beaten him entirely.

"Why are you using two in each cell? Are they that unreliable?"

Vanross glanced at him, a mocking smile on his lips. "They've been pretty reliable till now."

Joseph frowned. "You've used them before?"

Vanross nodded. His smile widened into a malicious grin. "Oh yes. We used them on your father's airship."

An explosion of rage drove Joseph to his feet, the folding metal chair dangling behind him. He charged at Vanross, screaming and bellowing, scarcely aware of what he was saying, wanting only to strike out and cause pain and suffering. Vanross watched him coolly, neatly sidestepping his charge, and clubbed him on the temple with the pistol again. Joseph went down heavily, unable to catch his fall with his bound hands, and a sharp pain in his shoulder vied with the unfolding flower of agony in his head, and then there was nothing.

THIRTY-SIX

IONE

The sound of Joseph crashing to the deck cut through her stupor.

"You've killed him!" She heard an hysterical edge in her voice, as if it were someone else screaming.

Blake glanced at her, shrugging. "Unlikely. But we're not hanging around to find out. I've got to get off this flying bomb before she goes up, and you're coming with me. A little insurance policy against any interference from Thornton's men." He stepped behind her and untied her hands, then jerked her to her feet. She could feel the muzzle of the little pistol pressing into the small of her back, hard and cold. "Let's go."

He propelled her roughly along the corridor and then into one of the passages that led between the two concentric corridors. Midway along it was a door. He hustled her through the door and up the stairs, two flights, and then out into a long, straight corridor which stretched away into the distance. The pressure of the pistol at her back was relentless, driving her forward, and she felt like crying, but she knew she had to stand up to him, somehow.

"You'll never get away with this, you know." She slowed down deliberately.

"Shut up and walk faster." The pistol jabbed painfully into her ribs. She tried to slow down again, but Blake simply increased the pressure, until she gasped from the pain, and she had to speed up again.

"That's better."

OK, so force isn't working. He's too strong. Try something else.

"Why are you doing this, Blake? After everything my father's done for you. How could you?"

Blake snorted. "Everything Howard Hughes has done for me has been out of guilt."

She was flabbergasted. "Guilt? For what?"

"For what happened to my father."

"What do you mean? Your father committed suicide, after he was found embezzling money from Toolco."

The gun jabbed into her savagely, and she nearly stumbled. "He wasn't an embezzler! Your grandfather framed him. Your father knew it. That's why he took me in, gave me an education and a job. But I always knew that one day I would have my revenge."

Ione could scarcely believe what she was hearing. "He took you in because he believed that the sins of the father should not be visited on the son! He wanted to give you a chance. He trusted you, and now you are betraying that trust in the most horrible way."

"Shut up, Ione. Thank God I won't have to listen to your whining voice much longer. Don't tempt me to make it even sooner."

He pulled her roughly towards a door in the corridor, opening it with his gun hand, and pushing her into a sort of lobby. There were lift doors in the right hand wall, and he pressed the call button to go up.

"Where are you taking me?"

Blake smiled thinly. "I already told you. We're getting off this deathtrap. There's a friend waiting with an airship up on deck." The lift arrived, and he hustled her into it, pressing the button for Main Deck. The doors closed and the lift began to rise. Ione watched the indicator apprehensively until they reached the top. It seemed to take an age for the lift to make its way up the shaft. Blake fidgeted impatiently at her side.

At last the lift ground to a halt, and the doors opened onto bright sunlight. She tried to shield her eyes against the glare, but Blake impatiently pushed her forwards and out of the lift. She stumbled on the threshold and fell to her knees. Blake cursed, and tried to yank her roughly to her feet, but she managed to wrap her arms around his ankles, immobilising him. He swore violently and tried to kick his legs free. She hung on grimly, pushing against his knees with her shoulder, and with a shout of anger, he went over, falling heavily onto his back. The gun went skittering across the deck and out of his reach.

She jumped to her feet as he lay there, winded and unable to draw breath or move, panic in his eyes. She scampered across the deck, picked up the gun, and walked back to Blake, ending up standing over him, with the gun pointing at his heart.

He raised his head and looked up at her apprehensively. "You ever shot a gun before?"

"Sure have. Daddy's taken me shooting a bunch of times." She tried to make herself sound as confident as possible, because the truth was that it had only been the once, and with a .22 rifle, not a pistol. She wasn't sure where the safety was on the little pistol, or whether the hammer needed to be cocked before it would fire. And had Blake already loaded a cartridge into the chamber?

As if reading her mind, Blake said "Can't remember if I actually loaded the thing or not." He gave a self-deprecating grin, then his eyes narrowed speculatively. "And it sure looks like you haven't taken the safety off."

It's a trick. Don't listen. She kept her eyes on him. "If you feel you can make your move without getting shot, by all means go ahead." She tightened her grip on the gun and steadied her aim.

Blake stared back at her for a long moment, his body

tense, and she held her breath, steeling herself to shoot if he made a sudden move. But after what seemed like an age, he let his breath out in a whoosh and slumped back against the deck, and relief flooded into her. *Well done, Ione! Now you know the gun is ready to shoot.* The knowledge was sobering, tempering her feeling of triumph, and she made sure to keep her finger resting on the trigger guard and not the trigger itself, the way her father had shown her. *Don't touch the trigger until it's time to shoot.*

"So what's your next move, Ione?" His tone was needling, but there was no mistaking the defeat in his posture.

"I'm taking you to Security HQ." *Be decisive, and show him you're in control.* She stepped back a few paces, so that she could cover him as he got to his feet. "Get up and get going."

But Blake simply lay there, completely unresponsive.

"Get up, Blake! I'm warning you, don't try me." She heard a shrill edge in her voice. *Be careful, Ione. If he thinks you won't do anything, you'll have lost control.*

By this time he had actually closed his eyes. The sight made her furious, because he was underestimating her. She suddenly knew what to do, and she walked quietly towards him, feeling her confidence building with every step.

She knelt down carefully. While holding the gun near to his ear, she cocked the hammer in one swift movement of her thumb. Blake's eyes flew open in alarm. She stepped back with alacrity and trained the gun on him again.

"Are you going to take me seriously now?"

"All right, Ione, you win." He let his breath out in a big sigh.

"Well, then. Get up! Let's go to Security HQ."

Blake groaned, and rolled laboriously onto his side, facing away from her. His posture was one of a man defeated. She relaxed, and waited for him to rise to his feet. But instead he sprang to his feet and started sprinting towards the nearest airship, which was a dilapidated old wreck sitting on a landing pad a few hundred yards away.

Blake's move was so sudden and so unexpected that several seconds ticked by before Ione could react. "Stop or

I'll shoot!" She shouted as loudly as she could, but Blake didn't look back or even break stride. She shook her head in frustration and anger, and slipped her finger inside the trigger guard. *It's now or never. Before he gets further away. You have to do it.* She aimed carefully at Blake's retreating back, and squeezed the trigger as smoothly as she could.

Nothing happened. The trigger moved about half-way through its action and then seemed to reach a stop. The safety must have been on. By this time Blake was nearly a hundred yards away, and she doubted that anyone could shoot a handgun accurately over such a distance. She lowered the pistol in frustration and watched helplessly as Blake got away.

THIRTY-SEVEN

JOSEPH

Someone was calling his name, someone far away, and he wished they would stop. He fought his way up to consciousness, and as he opened his eyes, the light seemed to flare the pain in his temple from a dull ache to a blinding throb, and he closed them again and groaned.

"Joseph! It's me, Harry! What happened to you?"

He opened his eyes more cautiously, rubbing his wrists, which ached abominably. He was lying on his back next to a metal chair. Harry was bending over him, concern and confusion on his open face.

The last moments of consciousness came back to him in a rush, and he sat up quickly, looking around him. This caused a spike of pain through his head, and he nearly cried out, hunching his shoulders as if to ward off the blow.

"Where are Ione and Vanross?"

Harry frowned. "I was with Miss Hughes before we decided to split up. I ain't seen Mr Vanross at all."

Joseph nodded wearily, forcing himself to get to his feet. He felt dizzy and nauseous, but the sight of the detonators embedded in the gas bag envelopes drove him to action. He turned to face his friend.

"Harry, this is very important. Aeropolis is in grave danger, and it's up to us to save her!" He explained what Vanross had told him about the detonators, and Harry's face drained of colour as he listened. He turned and ran to the nearest detonator, examining it closely.

"Don't touch it!" Joseph made his way slowly over to join him. Up close, the detonator made a ticking noise.

Harry's face was a picture of concentration as he stared at the stub of the detonator embedded in the fabric of the gas cell. "Well, we've got to try to do something. If we don't, it'll go up anyway. So we've nothing to lose by touching it."

Joseph had to admit that the logic was correct, but he felt himself cringe away from the little tube as Harry reached out a tentative hand. He held his breath as Harry gently took hold of it just below the knurled knob, and tried to twist it in its hole.

Nothing happened, and both of them released their held breaths cautiously.

"It feels stuck in there quite solid."

"There are barbs, pointing backwards, in a ring just below where you grabbed it," said Joseph. "They must have caught in the cloth of the envelope."

Harry frowned. "So that means we can't pull it back out again. At least, not without ripping the gas envelope to shreds."

Joseph felt hope draining away again. If they ripped the envelope, hydrogen would come pouring out, escaping into the access passageways, and it would only be a matter of time before a spark or a flame ignited it. And it would asphyxiate them as well. "So there's nothing we can do."

"Well, we can't pull it out. But we could push it all the way in," said Harry.

Joseph stared at him. "What good would that do?"

"If we could get it turned around inside there, we could pull it out the other way. The barbs must fold down when it's going forward."

"But we can't get inside the gas envelope. Can we?" Joseph

looked hopefully at the young apprentice.

Harry shook his head. "No, we'd die from lack of oxygen. But I've got some string." He pulled out a length of stout twine from his tool-belt. "We could tie it around the base of the knurled knob here, so when we push the detonator through the hole, we can pull it back up again."

It sounded desperately unlikely to Joseph. But he couldn't think of anything else to do. "It's worth a try, I suppose. What do we have to lose?"

"Nothing." Harry tied the twine tightly around the base of the detonator, then pushed it slowly and carefully until it was entirely through the hole, keeping the twine taut. The detonator dropped down gently into the void of the gas envelope, coming to rest against the inside of the fabric, just below the hole, with only the knurled knob visible.

Harry produced a pair of needle-nosed pliers from his tool-belt, and grasped the barrel of the detonator through the hole. By angling the pliers downwards and gently pulling up on the twine, he managed to work the jaws of the pliers down the barrel until they were grasping the spike at the end of the detonator. He carefully rotated the detonator until the spike protruded through the hole, so that he could get a grip on it with his fingers. After that it was nothing more than a slow pull through the hole, and the rest of the detonator soon followed. With a triumphant smile, Harry handed it to Joseph, and it lay in his palm, ticking softly.

He found one of the caps that Vanross had discarded, and screwed it back on, but this did not disarm it as he had hoped. In the meantime Harry had found some rags, and was using one to stuff into the hole left by the detonator, to slow the escape of the hydrogen.

Joseph looked at his friend, frowning. "That was very well done. But I'm sorry to say that there are five more detonators to take care of."

Harry nodded, and got to work on the next one. Joseph was feeling a lot less dizzy and the pain in his head was down to a dull ache. But he felt useless watching Harry at work. There was nothing he could do to help: Harry had only one pair of pliers.

Joseph made up his mind. "You've got things well in hand here. I'm worried about what Vanross has done with Ione. I'm going to try to find them."

Harry nodded. "If he's gone and taken her with him, he must be trying to get off Aeropolis. You should probably get to the main deck." He frowned. "Although it might be too late by now."

His words were like a dagger to Joseph's heart. "I have to try!" he shouted over his shoulder as he ran off along the corridor, trying to retrace his steps. He took the first passage off the curved corridor, and managed to find a staircase leading upwards. It emerged onto a landing that gave out onto a familiar-looking corridor. He tried to remember when he had seen it before. And then it came to him.

He ran down the corridor towards the glimmer of daylight that he could see at its end, and emerged onto a walkway that encircled an open space. The airshaft soared upwards above him. The mesh was anchored just below the railing that guarded the walkway. Beneath the mesh, a fan turned lazily. He looked at it with a shiver of recognition.

Then he jumped over the railing and made his way across the mesh to the very centre, lying down flat on his stomach, willing the fan to start up in earnest.

The seconds ticked by, and he began to think that he hadn't been as clever as he had thought in choosing this method of getting onto the main deck. *If I'd found a lift, I could be half-way up by now!*

Just as he decided to get up, the fan blades began to whip by below him with more urgency, and very soon the updraft began to blow his hair and clothing. In seconds he had lifted off, and was soaring up the airshaft, the lower decks flashing by.

I just hope the fan carries on spinning long enough to get me all the way to the surface.

The walls of the shaft were growing brighter, and before long he was bathed in shafts of sunlight. He craned his head up as far as he dared to try to see the top of the shaft, but suddenly he was out, in full sunlight, and the deck itself was below him. He was hovering high above it: as the air spilled out of the shaft and over the deck it seemed to be only strong enough to hold him up, not lift him any further. He manoeuvred himself cautiously, trying to orient before landing.

There was a man running towards him. With a shock of recognition, Joseph realised it was Vanross. He had his head down, intent on a destination behind Joseph, and didn't seem to have noticed the figure hovering some twenty feet above the level of the deck. Joseph frowned, and shifted his arm position so that he began to drift towards the edge closest to Vanross's path.

As he did so, he felt the airflow below him begin to falter. *The fan must be slowing down!* He fought down the panic and pulled in his arms even more, speeding up his forward motion. He shot over the edge of the shaft, still about ten feet off the deck, and dropped right on top of Vanross, who went down like a nine-pin, breaking Joseph's fall nicely.

THIRTY-EIGHT

IONE

By the time she reached the two of them, Joseph was already standing, looking a bit shaky, although Blake was still lying flat on the deck, cheek bleeding from a graze. He stared at her balefully as she raised the gun.

"You don't know how to use that, remember?"

She clicked the safety off. "I do now." She'd realised what the lever next to the hammer was for. Blake tightened his mouth, but remained otherwise motionless.

Joseph smiled broadly at her, and made as if to approach her. She shifted her aim to cover him. "Don't even think about it, Joseph."

The shock on his face seemed almost genuine. "What do you mean? I was just going to join you!" He gestured at Blake. "I stopped him running away, remember?"

She shook her head. "No. You were trying to join him, and messed up your... flying, or whatever that was you were doing. You knocked him over by accident."

"No, Ione, that's not true! Well, it probably was an accident, but I wasn't trying to join him—"

"Shut up, Joseph!" The hurt from his betrayal came out as

197

furious anger. "I don't want to hear your lies anymore! You brought those… detonators onto Aeropolis, you offered to help Blake before, and now you're trying to help him to escape. On that ship." She gestured at the dilapidated ship standing about a hundred yards away. "But I'm not going to let you."

As if on cue, the engines of the ship started up, and then she struggled laboriously into the air. Blake watched her go, then closed his eyes, seeming to deflate. But Joseph continued to look at her with his hurt, confused eyes. It was really annoying.

"But you saw me attack Vanross, when he admitted killing my father—"

"I said, be quiet!" She frowned. She didn't fully understand why Blake had had him tied up, and had admitted killing Joseph's father. But it must have been some sort of trick to confuse her when she suddenly showed up, so that Blake could overpower her. She was saved from further consideration of the difficulty by the arrival of Thornton and his troopers. Two of them covered Joseph and Blake as Thornton himself approached cautiously.

"What's going on here, Ione?"

Without taking her eyes off the two wrongdoers, she explained all that had happened in the gas envelope access corridors. When she had described the detonators and what Blake had done with them, Thornton held up his hand and called a trooper over. After receiving orders given to him in low, urgent tones, the man turned and ran back to the Core. Then Thornton turned back to her.

"I understand why you are holding Vanross. But what has Joseph done?"

She narrowed her eyes. "He brought the detonators onto Aeropolis."

Thornton turned to Joseph. "Is this true?"

Joseph gave him a stricken look, then dropped his gaze, and nodded.

"All right, we'll take it from here." He turned to a tall trooper whose hair was nothing more than blond stubble.

"Cole, take Mr Vanross and Master Samson to the brig, please. Ione, I think I'd better have that pistol now."

She turned to face him, handed him the gun, and then stalked off without a backward glance. She wasn't really crying. It was just the wind on deck, making her eyes water.

THIRTY-NINE

JOSEPH

He found himself walking in a partial daze, at the centre
of a circle of six troopers. Cole was at his elbow, pushing him
along, Vanross silent beside him. As they entered the Core he
was the subject of curious stares from bystanders, and he felt
a deep shame welling up inside him, making him want to
hide his face, ward off their accusing gaze.

*It's what I deserve. Although I never intended to, I've brought terrible
danger to their midst.*

The image of Ione, levelling the pistol at him, despising
him with her eyes, tore at his heart. He wiped his eyes on the
cuff of his shirt, wincing from the pressure on his temple.

The troopers stopped in front of the lifts. Cole pressed the
button. The first lift to arrive was one of the small ones. After
a moment's hesitation, Cole propelled Joseph into the car,
motioning one of the other troopers, a short ginger-haired
fellow, to bring Vanross in as well. He ordered the rest of the
squad to follow in the next lift, and hit the button for
Security HQ's level.

As soon as the doors closed, Vanross slumped against the
side wall of the car, groaning. The troopers ignored him, but

he turned to the ginger-haired one, a pleading expression on his face.

"Help me," he gasped, holding his abdomen. "I think he must have burst something inside me, when he fell on me." He pointed at Joseph, then doubled over, gagging and retching. The troopers automatically jumped back, and Vanross sprang to his right, as quick as a striking snake, and hit the emergency stop button. The lift shuddered to a halt, bringing everyone to their knees but Vanross, who had been ready for it, and he dropped into a crouch instead. Darting forward, he grabbed the sidearm out of Cole's holster, and then clubbed him viciously across the temple with it. The man fell headlong and was still. Vanross had the gun pointing at the other trooper's head before he could even rise off the floor.

"Don't move an inch."

The trooper stared at him, swallowed, then nodded reluctantly. Vanross moved backwards to the button panel, covering the trooper with the gun, and released the emergency stop. The lift began to move downwards again, and with a quick glance at the indicator, he hit the button for the next level. The lift moved smoothly to a stop, and the doors opened.

"Get out." Vanross motioned with the gun. "Pick him up, and take him out. Joseph, help him."

Together, Joseph and the trooper lifted Cole by the arms, and dragged him out of the lift. Vanross remained inside. The doors closed, and the lift indicator showed the lift moving upwards.

"He's going back up."

"What?" The trooper sounded distracted as he bent over Cole, trying to get a response from the stricken man.

"Vanross. He's going back up again."

"Well, obviously. He's going back to the deck to try and escape."

"But his ship took off. The *Lotus Flower*— I saw it take off. It's not on the deck." The trooper wasn't listening, but Joseph suddenly knew where Vanross was headed. He turned and looked up and down the corridor. *That way.* He set off at a run.

"Hey!"

Joseph stopped, and turned around. The trooper was staring at him. "You're still under arrest!"

"Do you really think Vanross would kick me out of the lift if we were working together?"

The man looked uncertain. "I suppose not. But what will I say to Thornton?"

Joseph shrugged. "Say that I escaped too. Oh, and tell him to send gunships to the aerial platform. The one on the very top of Aeropolis."

The trooper opened his mouth to protest, but Cole chose that moment to utter a moan, causing him to turn his attention away, and Joseph returned to his run down the corridor.

He found the shaft with the hollow column in the centre easily enough, and soon he was in the little cage, willing it to go faster as it was hoisted up the centre of the column. Then he was on the stairways, pounding his way upwards, and finally at the base of the ladder that led out into the exterior. He started climbing the ladder up the side of the column, and as he emerged he knew immediately that he had guessed right. The imposing bulk of an airship blocked out the sunlight above him, and from the uneven rumbling of her engines and her general state of disrepair, he knew she was the *Lotus Flower.*

Approaching with her gondola level with the platform that topped the column, her envelope had already bent or broken a number of the radio antennae that were bolted to the slender mast that rose from the centre of the platform. And clinging to that mast, watching the approaching airship, was Vanross.

Joseph swarmed up the ladder as quickly as his tired arms and legs could carry him, but even as he neared the top, the gondola drew abreast of the platform, its door standing open, and he saw Monmouth leaning out, a hand extended to help Vanross off the platform and onto the ship.

Joseph knew he wasn't going to make it in time. An impotent rage seized him as he watched Vanross step effortlessly off Aeropolis and safely onto the airship, and he heard the engine note increase as the pilot began to pull away.

Something struck him on the shoulder, and he clung to the ladder, heart pounding, but it was only one of the mooring ropes of the *Lotus Flower*, trailing behind her like the tentacles of a jellyfish. The rope moved over his shoulder, rubbing against it, and he was suddenly seized by the craziest idea he had ever had. He knew that if he thought about it for a second, he wouldn't do it, so he grabbed the rope with both hands, and let himself be pulled off the ladder.

FORTY

As he dangled from a rope below the airship, hundreds of feet above the earth, with Aeropolis being left rapidly behind, Joseph had to fight down the panic. Part of him was shouting angrily at himself for being a complete idiot, while another part was convinced he was going to die. He glanced downwards, at the green patchwork quilt of the home counties far below, and was hit by a wave of vertigo. He resolved to never do that again, and forced his gaze upwards, to his lifeline extending away above him, terminating at the airship, and he knew that his only hope was to climb.

Hand over hand he inched painfully up the rope, until his muscles burned and his shoulders ached with the strain. He discovered after a while that if he pressed his shoes together with the thick rope between them, he was able to get some traction, and with the aid of his leg muscles he made much better progress. Soon enough he was at the level of the gondola windows, and he saw, through them, Vanross and Monmouth and Rasmussen, all sitting together in the cockpit.

The sight filled him with anger. He suddenly wanted them to see him, so that they would know that they hadn't escaped, that he was still chasing them. His anger burned inside him, but even as his mind tried to come up with a way to get their attention, a cold realisation of how pathetic he would look came upon him. What could he do to them, dangling out here on the end of a rope? All they would have to do was remain aloft for a few hours, and he would fall, unable to cling on any longer.

But perhaps they had planned a long flight anyway? They were presumably fleeing Britain. A vision of falling into the cold dark water of the English Channel popped into his head, and he shuddered. *Maybe if they see me, they'll find some way to bring me in.* Being captured was preferable to dying. He wrapped one arm around the rope and began desperately fumbling in his jacket pockets with the other, looking for something that he could throw to get their attention. He had found nothing, and was feeling the panic starting to rise again, when his fingers closed around the first of the detonators that Harry had removed. He had slipped it into his pocket before he went after Ione and Vanross, and forgotten about it completely.

An idea came to him. He would just need something else. His questing fingers closed around a heavy brass object, and he realised that he still had the hotel key on its heavy fob in his pocket. Then he knew exactly what he was going to do.

He removed the key fob from his pocket, and threw it as hard as he could at the nearest gondola window. It smashed straight through and disappeared, leaving a jagged hole. After a few moments, Vanross appeared behind the window. He looked at the hole, then bent down, and came up holding the key fob, astonishment on his face. He looked up through the hole, straight at Joseph.

Joseph waved.

Vanross disappeared, and returned a moment later with Monmouth. The two of them stared out at Joseph. He took the detonator from his pocket, and showed it to them. Then he pointed up at the gas bag above his head.

Monmouth's expression turned from astonishment to fear, but Vanross flew into a rage, and began yelling obscenities, although Joseph could only hear them faintly over the engine noise. He smiled. Their reactions confirmed what he had already suspected: an airship as poorly maintained as the *Lotus Flower* would not have helium in her gas cells. It was hydrogen above him. He put the detonator into his pocket, and resumed his climb.

A few minutes later he was at the very top of the rope, where it was connected to a steel ring which projected out through the envelope from an internal rib. The fabric of the envelope was in reach. Wrapping his left arm around the rope again, Joseph carefully removed the detonator from his pocket, held it up, and then removed the cap, which was quite tricky to do one-handed. There was a heart-stopping moment when he almost dropped the detonator, but he snatched it up before it fell beyond his reach.

After collecting his wits, he took a firm grip on the detonator and drove it into the fabric above his head. The spike penetrated easily, and once he had pushed the body far enough in, the barbs caught in the weave, holding it firmly in place.

He glanced down at the gondola again. Monmouth must have been observing him with a pair of field glasses, because he dropped them as he disappeared from view. Moments later, Joseph felt his stomach lurch as the airship began a rapid descent. This steepened into a dive, and the green and pleasant land below was suddenly rushing up to meet them.

Joseph willed his aching fingers to hold on just a bit longer, as the patchwork quilt of fields and hedges loomed larger and larger. Rasmussen was apparently aiming for a large parklike expanse of soft rolling ground, surrounded by woods, and the *Lotus Flower* came shooting in over a low hill, engines screaming, and made the hardest landing Joseph had ever experienced. The impact jolted him from his rope, and he fell heavily onto soft grass. He rolled immediately to his feet and began to run away from the stricken airship. When he reached the tree line, he stopped, and turned back to see what was happening.

Vanross was staggering across the grass, blood streaming

across his face from a head wound. Monmouth stood with his back to Joseph, apparently remonstrating with Rasmussen, who seemed to be trying to jump up from the ground to reach the detonator. After a few moments, Monmouth gave up, and turned to trudge after Vanross. Seconds later, the gas envelope exploded with a deafening report, knocking Monmouth and Vanross flat, and leaving Joseph's ears ringing. When he looked up again, the airship was nothing but a blackened skeleton of girders on top of a smouldering gondola, scraps of envelope clinging to it here and there, burning fiercely. A thick column of dark smoke was rising lazily into the afternoon sky.

The deep bass notes of heavy aero engines made Joseph turn to look behind him, just as two airships breasted the hill and skimmed down over the treetops. Ropes unfurled from their gondolas and uniformed troopers rappelled down to land on the valley floor. Joseph recognised their leader. He watched Clive Thornton jog over to where Monmouth and Vanross lay, and then he turned, and slipped away into the woods.

FORTY-ONE

He stood outside the Chairman's office, straightened up, and knocked.

"Come in." Churchill's voice carried clearly through the thick oak. Joseph pushed the door open, and entered.

"Ah, good morning, young man. Come in, please sit down."

He crossed the Persian carpet and took a seat in the left hand visitor's chair.

"Miss Honeywell said that you wanted to see me, sir?"

Churchill cleared his throat. "Yes, I did. It's about this business with the banker's draft." He nipped the end off a cigar, and lit it, puffing slowly. "Dreadful thing, you know. Most unfortunate."

"Yes, sir. Although it has nothing to do with me."

The Chairman regarded him from beneath a raised eyebrow. "Nothing? Do I need to remind you that the draft was found in your pigeon hole, and made out to yourself?"

Joseph felt his cheeks colour. "No, sir. I know that, sir. What I meant was, I didn't put it there, and I certainly didn't make it out to anyone, let alone myself."

"Oh, I know *that*. No-one, and certainly not a bright

young man such as yourself, would be stupid enough to make out a draft in their own name. Also, the block letters are a bit of a giveaway, yes? No, the problem I face is that too many people know of the draft's existence. I must take action, otherwise people will talk, and nothing is more damaging to a bank's confidence than innuendo and rumour. So I need to fire Cooper. Show the City that we won't stand for any hint of malfeasance."

Joseph nodded. He was with the Chairman there— no doubt in his mind that Mickey needed to go. But Churchill seemed to have something else on his mind as well. He leaned forward in his chair, looking directly into Joseph's eyes. His face showed concern, and regret.

"But I need to do more." He sighed. "I want you to know that I've thought long and hard about this, but unfortunately I can't see any other way of resolving the situation satisfactorily. I don't want to let any lingering doubts remain over this business."

Joseph's heart sank. This sounded like very bad news indeed.

"I need to let you go too."

Even though he had been dreading it since the start of this whole business, it was still an enormous shock. It hit him like a physical blow in the stomach, leaving him feeling weak and breathless. What would he tell his mother? How would he provide for her?

Churchill was still looking at him, concern in his eyes. "I really am sorry about this, Joseph." He managed a half-smile. "But, do you know what, I suspect that it may turn out for the best. I know that you're not very happy here. And, I happen to know someone who is looking for a new employee."

He rose from behind his desk, and Joseph followed him to the door which led to his private ante-room. Opening it, he motioning to Joseph to go through. There was a man standing with his back to them, looking out of the window. He turned around as Churchill quietly closed the door.

"Hello, Joseph."

Joseph was too surprised to say anything for a moment. Howard Hughes walked towards him, smiling broadly.

"I sure am glad to see that you got away from Monmouth and Vanross in one piece. Until I heard from Mr Churchill, we were a bit worried about you."

Joseph found his voice. "Yes, sir, I did... manage to get away. I— I'm sorry I didn't make myself known to Mr Thornton. After the explosion."

"Oh, that's all right. I guess you weren't too sure how welcoming he'd be! Don't blame you at all." A wry smile appeared on his face. "That explosion sure was something, wasn't it? Saw it from one of our airships. I guess someone gave Monmouth a taste of his own medicine."

Joseph could feel the colour rising in his cheeks again, but before he could say anything, Hughes continued.

"On the other hand, it's a wonder such a shabby old wreck managed to fly for so long without exploding. That's what we're telling the authorities, anyway. Seems like the least complicated option." He gave a quick wink, then his face became more serious.

"But I know what you did to save Aeropolis. Young Harry told us all about what you two did down in the gas envelope galleries. That was mighty quick thinking, and if you hadn't done it..." Hughes trailed off, shaking his head.

"So I wanted you to know that I appreciate what you did. Ione now, she did what she thought was right, so I don't apologise for her, and you have to admit it was pretty dumb to bring those detonators on board." Joseph opened his mouth to protest, but Hughes held up his hand. "I believe that you didn't know what they were. I'm just saying, if you'd have come straight to me with them, you wouldn't have ended up on the wrong side of Ione's gun! Anyways, all's well that ends well, as the poet says."

"How is Ione?"

Hughes smiled ruefully. "She's OK. On her way back to the States. She's still pretty darned annoyed with you, though. My daughter ain't the forgivin' type, I'm afraid. But give it time, she'll come around."

Joseph nodded, though it wasn't what he'd hoped to hear. Still, it was more positive than he'd feared. He didn't get much time to think about it, though, because Hughes wasn't finished.

"Now, you may not know of this, but your father was gonna leave the Zeppelin company and come to work for me. It was all arranged, he was just doing the one final test flight for them." He frowned. "I always knew the explosion was no accident. The ZA don't take kindly to what they see as betrayal.

"Anyway, I've been talking to Andy Rowan, about your little flight in the Spitfire. To tell you the truth, I didn't get much choice about it, he pretty much demanded to speak with me! He wants you in the Air Corps. And I've been thinking about it as well. I still want a Samson to work for me.

"What do you say, Joseph? Will you do it? Will you come and fly for me?"

Joseph stared at him, trying to process all the implications of what he was hearing. The thought of going back to Aeropolis, and actually living and working there, suddenly thrilled him. He remembered the feeling of soaring into the air in the Spitfire, and he longed to feel it again. The only cloud on the horizon was the thought of telling his mother. *She won't like it. Not at all.*

Well, it was his life after all. He was nearly a man. It was time for him to be true to his heritage. He stood up straight. *I love you, Dad. I won't let you down.*

Hughes was looking at him. "Do you need time to think about it? Talk it over with your mama, maybe?"

Joseph shook his head. "No, sir. I've decided. I want to do it!"

Hughes beamed at him. "Excellent!" He rubbed his hands together. "Well, let's go then. I'll run you home, you can pack a few things, and we'll be back on Aeropolis by noon. Come on!"

Joseph ran to catch up with the excitable American as he rushed out of the room. *This is going to be amazing.*

AUTHOR'S MESSAGE

Thanks for reading, I hope you enjoyed it! If you did, I would be very grateful if you would leave a review of the book on Amazon, to help others decide whether the book is right for them.

I'd love to hear from you on my website, where you can also sign up to be notified when the next book in the Aeropolis sequence is available: don't worry, I won't abuse your email address! (You can unsubscribe at any time if you change your mind.)

Here's where to find me: www.StephenWest.net

All the best,

Stephen

ACKNOWLEDGEMENTS

Writing would mean nothing without readers. I would like to thank all of the people who have read my work, from those, like Ken and Elaine, who laboured through early drafts, catching typos and making valuable suggestions, to those, like you, who have paid money for the finished article. To all of you, I give my gratitude.

Most of all, I would like to thank my wonderful wife Louisa, for reading draft after draft, for supporting me through the long process of bringing a first novel to publication, and for always believing in me.

Stephen West

ABOUT THE AUTHOR

STEPHEN WEST is an ex-pilot and flying enthusiast who was born and raised in South Africa. Since moving to London he has worked in finance. *Airship City* is his first novel and the first in a series of books about Joseph Samson's adventures on the amazing Aeropolis. He lives in a small town just outside London with his family. Find out more about Stephen at www.StephenWest.net or follow him on Twitter @StephenWest.

Made in the USA
Charleston, SC
29 May 2014